Truth Be Told

Charles Huss

Published by Charles Huss, 2025.

This is a work of fiction. Similarities to real people, places, or events are entirely coincidental.

TRUTH BE TOLD

First edition. June 9, 2025.

Copyright © 2025 Charles Huss.

ISBN: 979-8999194800

Written by Charles Huss.

For my mom, Nancy, who is not only a great proofreader, but also a great mom and the most likable person I know.

Chapter 1

Peter Beckett hesitated before the confessional. The ornate wooden box was supposed to liberate one from the sins of the flesh, but it felt more like a judgmental parent. He had been here many times over the last twenty-five years, and it felt the same each time.

Ever since he woke up one evening, confused and disoriented in front of St. Bertilla Catholic Church in Milwaukee, this place has felt like a second home. Father Aziel, a young priest at the time, noticed him and brought him inside. He brewed a pot of coffee and gave him a place to sleep it off. It soon became clear Peter had no memories of who he was or where he came from.

Over the years, he had grown accustomed to his situation but never entirely accepted it. Whenever he was feeling down, he would come to church to talk about it. It wasn't always in the confessional, but Father Aziel took confessions on Saturdays. He tried therapy, but no therapist ever lasted more than a few weeks, so he gave up on them and relied on advice from the priest. The advice never fixed his problem, but it did help him feel better for a while. The human contact, more than the advice, probably helped him the most, and since the priest wasn't bothered by what he was, he was the only person Peter could comfortably talk to.

He hesitated for a moment and then stepped inside. As he knelt, the partition slid open. After a short pause, Peter said, "Bless me, Father, for I have sinned. It has been several months since my last confession."

Father Aziel replied softly, "It is good to hear your voice again, Peter. Remember, no sin is too great for God's mercy. What have you come to confess?"

Through the screen, Peter could see that Father Aziel hadn't changed much since their first encounter. Unlike Peter, his hair was still thick and dark. Peter took a breath. "I took the Lord's name in vain," he said before exhaling. "No! I did worse than that. I cursed God. I told him I hated him for what he did to me."

There was a short pause that seemed to linger. Then, in a calm voice, Father Aziel asked, "Why are you angry with God, Peter?"

"You know why," Peter said, almost whispering.

Father Aziel sighed. "This has always troubled you. I understood why it bothered you when you were younger, but I had hoped you would eventually see it as a gift, not a curse. God gave you something remarkable. He has a plan for you. You should accept that you have your gift for a special purpose."

Peter clenched his fists. "I didn't ask for this so-called gift, and I don't want it. I'm a freak. People are afraid of being near me. You can't imagine what it's like to have people intentionally avoid you." Peter stopped talking when he realized his words came out loud enough for the people in the church to hear.

"You obviously don't understand the life of a priest. People avoid me quite often."

"Maybe some people, but not all people."

"Not all people avoid you, either, Peter. I am happy to talk to you."

"I appreciate that, Father, but it's not enough. You need to talk to God for me. He won't listen to me. Tell him to remove this curse."

"You don't need me to talk to God. You can talk to him yourself. He will listen to you. He may not answer you right away, but he will listen. God is with you now and always will be."

"Sorry, Father, but God being with me is not working. I need someone else to be with me. Preferably someone pretty and female that isn't bothered by what I am."

Father Aziel sighed again, "This is the house of the Lord, Peter, not a dating site. I will pray for you, but you must trust God's plan. Stop whining and use your gift the way God intended it to be used."

The priest's directness took Peter aback. "But... I don't know what God's intentions are."

"You will know if you keep your mind and heart open."

"It has been twenty-five years. If God had a plan for me, don't you think I would have found out by now?"

"God is not always in a hurry, Peter. Be patient. Eventually, your purpose will become clear." He said a short prayer, finishing with, "Go in peace, my son, and serve the Lord."

Peter emerged from the confessional, stepping into the cavernous church. He passed several parishioners, some of whom were kneeling in prayer, and made his way to the large wooden doors. Pushing them open, he stepped into the late summer heat. The sun felt good on his face as a warm breeze carried the scent of sizzling hot dogs from a nearby vendor. When he reached the main sidewalk, a woman jogger plowed into him. The collision sent them both sprawling onto the hard concrete.

After the initial shock of what had happened subsided, Peter stood and saw the woman sitting up, clutching her left shoulder. She was young, perhaps in her early to mid-twenties, with her long blond hair tied behind her head. She wore white tennis shoes, black shorts, and a pink tank top. Her baseball cap lay on the ground near Peter's feet. He picked it up and then offered his hand to the woman. She accepted, and he pulled her up, whereupon she continued clutching her left shoulder.

"Are you okay?" Peter asked as he handed her hat back.

"I'm great. Never better," she said as she put the hat back on her head.

Peter's eyes widened in shock, but he said nothing.

"I'm sorry," the woman said. "I jog here almost every day and have never run into anyone before. I guess I was distracted."

"It's okay," Peter said. "Are you sure you're okay? Maybe you should have that shoulder looked at."

The woman rubbed her shoulder again. "It's fine. I'll be okay."

"It's probably mostly my fault," Peter said. "I stepped onto the sidewalk without looking. Let me make it up to you. Can I buy you lunch? The guy across the street has great hot dogs."

"That is nice of you, uh...,"

"Peter. Peter Beckett."

"That is nice of you, Peter, but I'm not interested in starting a relationship right now."

"I'm twice your age," Peter said. "While I would be flattered if you were attracted to me, a relationship is not what I expected."

"I'm sorry. I need to get going."

"If you don't like hot dogs, he also sells Polish sausages."

"Thanks, but I really should go."

As she started to walk away, Peter asked, "Can you at least tell me your name?"

After hesitating, she turned and said, "It's Hannah."

"Just Hannah?"

"Hannah Meyers," she said before walking back in the direction she came from.

"Okay, Hannah Meyers," Peter called out. "Look me up if you change your mind."

Hannah smiled but said nothing and continued to walk away. Peter watched until she turned the corner and disappeared. He didn't notice the black van across the street pull out and follow her.

***

When the van reached Hannah Meyers, it pulled alongside her and screeched to a stop. The side door slid open, revealing what appeared to be a mobile surveillance center. Hannah stepped inside and closed the door. Two men were inside the van. The driver got out of his seat and stepped into the back of the vehicle. He was tall, around forty, and wore a black suit jacket with black pants and a white shirt. His gray tie prevented him from looking like a member of Men in Black. He stooped as he navigated through the cramped space to the back near Hannah.

At the same time, the other man, who opened the door for Hannah, returned to his seat in front of a control console in the back of the van. In front of him, several monitors displayed the area around the van. He was younger than the driver, perhaps thirty years old. He dressed similarly to the first man, but his tie was loose, and his jacket hung over his chair. He turned his chair so he could see Hannah.

The first man sat on a seat next to the other man, and Hannah sat across from them. "Okay, I lied to him. What did that accomplish?" she asked.

"You told him your real name. Why did you do that?" The first man asked.

"I don't know. I couldn't think of a fake name quickly enough. Don't forget, I also told him I jog here almost every day. I never jog anywhere near here."

"Maybe he can turn it on and off," the second man suggested.

"Turn what on and off?" Hannah asked.

"I think we need to monitor him a little longer. We need to know for sure," the first man said.

"Listen, Agent Carter, I was perfectly happy to work with you guys from Washington, but now I feel like a fool. This is a waste of time."

"It's not a waste of time, and since you didn't exactly volunteer to help us, you may as well get comfortable. Since we will be working together, perhaps we should drop the formalities. My name's Tim, and this is Ben. Can we call you Hannah?"

Hannah slowly nodded. "Yeah, sure."

"Okay, Hannah, here's the situation. I don't know how much your office told you about why we are here."

"They only told me we are trying to break up a drug ring. What I don't understand is why the FBI is investigating this instead of the DEA."

"I'm sure the DEA has this on their radar, but our interest is in the drug cartels. One of the largest has set up shop somewhere in Milwaukee and is probably planning on distributing fentanyl throughout the Midwest from here. Not only that, but this stuff is also more potent than usual. Overdoses in Milwaukee alone have spiked by over twenty percent in the last few weeks. Once these people fully establish this operation, we could be looking at a national tragedy."

"How are they getting the drugs into the country? I thought they had the border locked up tighter than a drum," Hannah said.

"You and I both know that's impossible. Our job is to learn how the drugs are getting in. We also need to find the head of the operation here. If this man, Peter, doesn't have the ability we think he has, our job will become much harder."

Hannah shook her head. "No. I won't help unless you tell me the whole truth. Why did you want me to lie to this guy? What ability do you think he has, and how do you know he has it?"

Tim nodded. "Okay. I don't see why you shouldn't know everything. We keep tabs on a lot of people that we consider, uh, shall we say, 'special.'" When he said the word "special," he made air quotes with his fingers. "It's a lucky coincidence that he lives in Milwaukee."

"Are you saying he has some kind of psychic ability?" Hannah asked. "You should know I don't believe in that paranormal stuff. I also don't believe in flying saucers, leprechauns, and Bigfoot."

"We're not talking about Bigfoot here," Tim said.

"What are we talking about?"

"He seems to be able to get the truth out of people," Ben said. "In other words, people can't lie to him."

"That's crazy. I lied to him. Where do you get your intel from?"

"You lying to him may have been an anomaly," Ben said. "We've had several credible reports that this guy is the real deal."

"What other kinds of people do you consider 'special'?" Hannah asked, also making air quotes.

"Well, a woman in California supposedly can sense earthquakes before they happen," Tim said. "A man in Florida can stay underwater for eight minutes, and a man in Maine seems abnormally tolerant to cold weather." He looked to Ben for more examples.

"What about that guy right here in Wisconsin who can heal people by touching them?"

"That's right," Tim said. "That one, I'm not so sure about. Anyway, the point is that billions of people are in this world. By pure chance, some of them will be special in one way or another."

Hannah nodded and said, "Okay. We'll watch him and test him again. If you're right, hopefully, he can help."

***

Peter lived in a modest home a few miles west of the downtown area. He pulled into the driveway and parked behind the pickup truck he used for his business. He didn't go inside right away when he got home. Instead, he opened the side door of his detached garage. The familiar scent of sawdust and machine oil greeted him when he stepped inside his woodworking shop. Dozens of hand tools hung from the walls while woodworking machinery occupied much of the perimeter. A large table stood in the center of the room. The only thing that seemed out of place was the bicycle that hung from the rafters. Peter picked up an electric sander and started sanding a dresser he was working on. After a few minutes, he changed his mind, put the sander away, and went into the house.

The wood floors creaked under his feet as he walked inside. A beautiful gray cat with deep, golden eyes greeted him near the door. The cat looked up and meowed several times before rubbing his cheek on Peter's leg.

"Okay, Sammy. Just a minute," Peter said as he walked to the kitchen. He emptied a can of cat food into a bowl and placed it on the floor in front of Sammy, who quickly began eating it.

Peter poured himself a glass of iced tea and carried it into the bedroom, where he had his computer desk. It was near a window overlooking his front yard. He had a bird feeder hanging from a tree in the yard. He put it there for Sammy, but he also enjoyed watching the variety of birds that would visit for a nice snack. The feeder also attracted an occasional squirrel, which Peter liked watching even more than the birds. Before sitting down, he looked out the window. He saw no birds on the feeder but noticed a large black van parked across the street. He had seen a similar van near the church but assumed there must be hundreds of them in the city.

He sat down at his desk and tapped a key on his keyboard. Two large monitors came to life. He typed "Hannah Meyers Milwaukee" in the search bar and hit enter. It returned more than a hundred thousand results. *It must be a common name*, he thought. He clicked on the images tab and scrolled through dozens of photos before finding her. He clicked through to a social media post saying she had been accepted to the FBI Academy.

He looked out the window and saw the van still parked across the street. He leaned back in his chair for a minute and then continued. He looked for more recent posts from Hannah, but that was the last one he found. It was dated almost eight months ago. So, she was a rookie. Now, he wondered if she had run into him accidentally or on purpose. He looked out at the van again and decided it was no accident.

He wondered what the point was. He had done nothing illegal. If he had, she would have arrested him on the spot. And how was she able to resist him? That had never happened before. Did she know about his so-called gift? Did she find a way to counteract it? If so, he needed to know more.

He deliberately avoided looking at the van across the street as he left his house. He turned left when he reached the sidewalk and walked to the corner. After crossing the street, he picked up his pace. He took his phone out of his pocket and looked at it. He didn't turn it on. Instead, he looked at the reflection on the screen. The van was following him. He smiled.

After another block, he stepped inside a coffee shop. It was a place he had visited often. The smell of fresh coffee hung in the air as he entered. The shop had an industrial look with a high ceiling and exposed air ducts. The floor was polished concrete, with several wooden tables and chairs arranged in rows. A couple of sofas lined the far wall. The counter was ahead and to the right. Several people stood in line to order coffee. About a dozen more sat at the tables, and a couple of women having a conversation sat on one of the sofas.

Peter stepped left and pressed himself against the wall near the door. Fifteen seconds later, Hannah walked in. She was still wearing her jogging clothes. She looked at the line and then at the people sitting at the tables.

"Looking for someone?" came Peter's voice from behind her.

Hannah turned, startled. "Oh, Peter. I changed my mind and looked you up like you said. I saw you leaving as I got to your house. I tried to catch up with you, but you were too fast."

"Cut the crap. I know you're following me. I also know you're with the FBI. What do you want from me?"

Hannah stumbled over her words. "Well, uh, I'm not really at liberty to say."

"I bet I know who is," Peter said, storming out the door.

He walked quickly to the van parked across the street and pulled open the driver's side door. "Who the hell are you?" he yelled at the driver. "What do you want with me?"

"I'm Special Agent Timothy Carter of the FBI," the driver said. He pointed at the man in the passenger seat and said, "This is Special Agent Benjamin Green. We are here to determine if you truly have the ability to force people to tell the truth. Now we know."

Hannah had caught up to Peter and stood next to him. He looked at her and said, "I don't force anyone to tell the truth. They do so willingly. Some more willingly than others, it seems."

Peter looked back at Tim Carter. "Now that you know, what is it you want?"

"We need your help. A major drug cartel has set up shop here in Milwaukee. Many people have already died, and we thought, with your help, we could find them and shut them down before more people needlessly lose their lives."

"Oh, so you think if I ask a bunch of people questions, somebody will spill the beans."

"That's right," Tim said.

"Sorry, but I'm not interested," Peter said before walking away.

Tim motioned for Hannah to follow him, which she did. When she caught up to him, she grabbed his arm and said, "Peter, wait!"

Peter stopped and looked at her. "I told you I'm not interested."

"I heard you the first time, but I don't understand. You have the ability to save hundreds, if not thousands, of lives. How could you not want to help?"

Peter started walking again. "I have my reasons."

Hannah kept pace with him. "What reasons?"

Peter stopped again. "Mostly, I can't think of anyone who deserves to be saved." He started walking again.

Hannah caught up to him again. "What do you have against humanity?"

Peter stopped again. He looked Hannah in the eyes and said, "I have nothing against humanity. It's humanity that doesn't like me."

"I like you," Hannah said.

Peter shook his head. "I don't know how you are able to lie to me, but it doesn't feel as good as I thought it would." He started walking again.

Hannah grabbed his arm again and said, "Wait! Please!"

Peter stopped and looked at her. "Okay, fine. If you like me, then have dinner with me tonight."

Hannah looked back at the van and then at Peter. "If I have dinner with you, will you help us?"

"No, but if you have dinner with me, you will have an opportunity to change my mind."

Hannah nodded. "Okay, but I don't like seafood."

"What about Italian?"

"That's perfect. I'll pick you up at six."

"No," Peter said. "I want to see where you live. Give me your address, and I'll pick you up at six."

Hannah hesitated, looked back at the van again, then took out her phone. "Okay, I'll text it to you. What's your number?"

Peter gave Hannah his phone number, and she texted him her address. He looked at it and said, "Oh, you're not far from here. It's a wonder I never ran into you before."

"Maybe if you weren't actively trying to avoid people, we might have met long ago."

"What makes you think I try to avoid people?"

"You work from home and hate humanity, but I get it. I wouldn't want to be around someone who always compelled me to tell the truth. I don't usually lie, but it would be like letting someone read my mind. People need a certain amount of privacy."

"I told you I don't hate humanity, and I don't blame people, but it still hurts to be rejected by everyone."

"So, you've never had a relationship with someone?"

"Yes, of course I have. Most people don't realize why they feel compelled to tell me the truth at first, but after a while, they put two and two together, and then they want to stay far away from me."

Hannah put her hand on Peter's arm and said, "I'm sorry. It must be tough for you."

"What is so special about you?" Peter asked. "Why can you lie to me?"

"I have no idea. They say that everyone has a soulmate." Hannah realized what she said and added, "Maybe soulmate is the wrong word. Maybe we are like counterparts."

"Okay, counterpart. I'll see you tonight."

"What happened?" Tim asked when Hannah returned to the van.

"I have a date with him tonight."

"A date? What about him helping us?"

"I don't know yet. I guess I'll know more after our date."

Chapter 2

There was no driveway at the address Hannah had given Peter, so a few minutes before six, he parked his car on the street in front of the house. It was an older, two-story home with similar homes very close on each side. Gates between the homes restricted access to the backyards.

Peter picked up the roses he had purchased on the way and got out of the car. He walked down the sidewalk and ascended the three steps to a large wooden porch. On either side of the stairs in front of the porch, small flower beds sat empty, devoid of plants. He rang the bell and waited. After fifteen seconds, the door opened. Hannah smiled when she saw Peter.

She wore a simple cream-colored dress that hugged her beautiful curves. Peter looked her up and down and said, "You look amazing." He then handed her the flowers. "I didn't know your favorite flowers, so I got you roses."

"Roses are perfect," Hannah said. "Come in. Let me put these in water."

Peter stepped inside and closed the door behind him. The old, hardwood floor creaked under his feet. It reminded him of his own home. He looked around as Hannah went into the kitchen with the flowers. Her home was spotless but relatively bare. It lacked character. The living room contained a sofa, a reclining chair, a coffee table, and an end table, but not much else. There was no television and no pictures on the wall. There was also no sign that she collected anything or had any hobbies.

"Did you just move in?" Peter asked.

"Is it that obvious?"

"Well, it looks a little sparse."

"Yeah, I rented it about two months ago. I've been filling it slowly when I have time and money. I was lucky to get assigned here. Everyone gets to choose a preferred location, but that choice is more like a wish, especially for rookies like me."

"Why did you choose Milwaukee? I mean, I probably would have picked someplace like Honolulu."

Hannah brought the vase of flowers from the kitchen and placed them on the dining room table. She looked at Peter and said, "You learned I was with the FBI. You must have also learned I grew up here."

"I assumed you grew up here, but I stopped looking once I saw you were with the FBI. That's when I led you to the coffee shop."

"What made you look me up in the first place? I'm not going to lie. It seems a little creepy."

"It's no more creepy than you looking me up. You were the first person who ever lied to me. I needed to know who you were and what made you special."

"I guess that makes sense, but I have no idea why I am different than others," Hannah said. "When I was assigned to work with Agents Carter and Green, I thought it was an opportunity to impress the higher-ups. Then, when I learned my primary job was to lie to some guy, I started to wonder whether I had chosen the right profession."

"Some guy?" Peter asked.

"You know what I mean. At the time, you were just 'some guy.' Then, when Agent Carter started talking about a list of special people, I really thought I was in the wrong profession. Now that I know you're real, I feel better about it."

"I shouldn't be surprised I ended up on someone's list. I think what surprises me most is that it took twenty-five years."

"That's government efficiency for you," Hannah said. "Would you like to go? I'm getting hungry."

"Of course," Peter said and opened the door.

They walked to Peter's car, and he opened the passenger door for Hannah.

"Oh, wow! Is this your car? It's beautiful," she said before sliding in.

"Yep, and it's all paid for," Peter said. He closed Hannah's door, walked around to the driver's side, and got in.

"How did you afford to buy a new Corvette?" Hannah asked.

"You mean you don't know? Didn't your FBI guys have me thoroughly checked out?"

"They probably did, but they didn't tell me everything. So, where did you get the money? I know you have no known relatives, so I'm pretty sure a rich uncle didn't die and leave it to you."

"No, it definitely did not come from a rich uncle. I don't even know who my real parents are."

After a brief pause, Hannah asked, "So, are you going to tell me or leave me hanging?"

Peter started the engine. It roared to life. He pulled out onto the street. He looked in the mirror and then at Hannah. "I'm surprised your friends aren't following us."

"Agent Carter wanted to keep an eye on us, but I made it clear that I'm a big girl who does not need his help."

"I think it's good that you are standing up for yourself as a rookie. A more timid person might be bringing those guys coffee."

"A more timid person wouldn't join the FBI."

"Good point."

"Do you not want to tell me about the car?"

"I don't mind telling you if you promise not to judge me."

"You're not going to tell me you did something illegal, are you?"

"Illegal? No. Not technically."

"What does 'not technically' mean?"

"Well, I went to Las Vegas last year and learned I'm very good at poker. So good that several casinos asked me not to return. Apparently, I'm bad for business."

Hannah looked at him briefly, smiled, and shook her head. "I should have known. Poker's a bluffing game."

Peter grinned but said nothing.

A few minutes later, they arrived at an Italian restaurant in a pedestrian-friendly area near downtown, between a coffee shop and a men's clothing store. Several tables were set up outside. The sun was low, and the building cast a long shadow over the tables. Peter opened the door for Hannah and followed her inside.

The air inside was rich with the aromas of garlic and basil, as well as the smell of freshly baked bread. "Good evening," the hostess said to them as they entered. "Is it just the two of you?"

"Yes," Peter said. "We have a reservation under Peter Beckett."

The woman looked down and said, "Oh, yes. I see you here. Would you like a table inside or outside?"

Peter looked at Hannah, who said, "I think outside would be nice."

"It's a beautiful evening," the hostess said. "Follow me."

She picked up two menus, led them back outside, and set the menus on a table. A young couple sat at a table beside them, but the other nearby tables were empty. "Your server will be with you shortly," she said before returning inside.

"This was a good choice," Hannah said. "I've been here a few times, and the food is always good. Plus, the weather is perfect for eating outside."

"I thought you would like it. I brought someone here once before. You can't imagine how hard it is to take a woman on a date and avoid asking her personal questions. They think you don't care about them."

"I can see where that would be a problem."

"Do you know what the worst part is? The more some of them think I don't care, the more interested they become in me. How messed up is that?"

"Everybody wants to be liked. I guess some people take rejection, or perceived rejection in your case, as a challenge."

"I suppose that's true."

"So, people only open up to you when you ask them questions? I mean, they don't feel compelled to confess their sins when you are around?"

"No. Thank God for small favors. They only want to answer the questions I ask them."

"Do you mean they can lie if you don't ask them a question?"

"Well, no. I haven't experienced that yet that I know of, but they can keep their mouth shut and not say anything."

"What about on the telephone? Can people lie on the phone?"

"Yes. The telephone is the only way I can have a normal conversation with someone without worrying about them telling me something they don't want to tell me."

"I think having your ability on the phone would be awesome. Imagine how nice it would be if the representative from the electric company told you the real reason why your electric bill was so high."

Peter laughed. "Yeah, I see your point. It would be better if my ability worked on the phone but not in person."

Their server arrived at the table. He was a young man of average height with thick, dark hair. He might have been of Italian descent, perhaps a son or grandson of the owners, but he was likely born and raised in the area, given his local accent. "Good evening," he said. "My name is Nick. I'll be your server tonight. Can I get you something to drink?"

Peter looked at Hannah. "Would you like a glass of wine?"

Hannah shook her head and looked at the server. "I'll have a sparkling water."

"I'll have the same," Peter said.

When the server left, Peter asked, "Do you think you're on duty now?"

"No, but I tend to talk too much when I'm drinking. I mean, I've been known to say stupid things."

"If you mean you speak your mind and tell people things they don't want to hear, then don't worry, I've heard it all."

The server brought their drinks a short time later and asked if they were ready to order.

"What is your favorite meal?" Peter asked him.

"I love the fettuccine alfredo. It's almost better than sex." He looked around and added, "I'm sorry. That just came out for some reason."

"It's okay," Peter said. "What is your least favorite meal?"

The server quickly glanced over his shoulder and whispered, "The ravioli tastes like SpaghettiOs."

Peter looked at Hannah, who said, "I happen to like SpaghettiOs."

Peter smiled at the server and said, "Well, I guess the young lady wants the SpaghettiOs."

Hannah laughed and shook her head. "No. I'll have the fettuccine alfredo."

"I'll have the same," Peter said before handing the server his menu.

When he left, Peter said, "What were we talking about? Oh, I remember. You talk too much when you drink. What about when you are not drinking? Are you more of a talker or a listener?"

"I would say I'm more of a listener. I'm not shy, but I'm also not the life of the party, if you know what I mean."

"I do indeed, but today, you have to be the talker. You are on a mission, after all."

"A mission? What do you mean?"

"You're on a mission to recruit me, aren't you? So, go ahead."

Hannah's eyes narrowed. "What?"

"Recruit me. Let me hear your sales pitch."

Hannah looked around the room and back at Peter. She said quietly, "I want to convince you to help us, but I'm here with you because I want to be here. I would have accepted your offer for a date even if you had already agreed to help us."

Peter leaned back in his chair and smiled. "This is so weird."

"What is so weird?"

"Trying to figure out if you are telling me the truth. How do you do it?"

Hannah folded her arms and looked away. She looked back at Peter angrily and said, "I'm going to overlook that comment because I know your circumstances are unusual, but you don't bring a woman on a date and then tell her you suspect she is lying to you."

"You're right," Peter said, looking down. He looked Hannah in the eyes and said, "Please forgive me. That was a stupid thing to say. I didn't mean to offend you."

"It's okay. If you want to know how normal people determine if someone is lying, certain mannerisms give it away. I learned a lot about that during my training, but in real-world situations, I tend to forget everything I learned and rely on instinct."

"Do you have a good instinct for detecting liars?"

Hannah took a drink of water and shook her head. "I suck at it," she said and laughed.

Peter smiled. "It sounds like you need help."

Hannah's face turned serious. "Are you saying you will help us?"

"I have conditions."

"Okay," Hannah said slowly. "What are your conditions?"

"I'll need to put my business on hold, so I want to get paid at least what I'm making now."

"I think that's reasonable. Anything else?"

"Yes. I want to work with you alone. Those other guys can be backup, but you must take the lead."

"That might be a hard ask," Hannah said. "I doubt Agent Carter will want to give up control, especially to a rookie."

"Tell him he can take it or leave it."

"Why do you want to work with only me? I mean, four heads are better than two."

"They can help, but from a distance. You are the first person I have felt comfortable talking to other than my priest. If those other agents spend too much time with me, one or both might say something they don't want to say. Then things will get awkward."

Hannah nodded. "I guess I can see that. Okay. I'll talk to the other agents and pick you up at nine if they are okay with it. Even if they're not okay with it, I'll ensure you get what you want."

The waiter returned with a basket of bread, butter, and two small plates. He set them on the table and said, "Your meals should be up shortly. Is there anything else I can get you?"

They both shook their heads and said, "No, thank you" simultaneously.

When the waiter left, they each removed a piece of bread from the basket. Hannah buttered her piece and pushed the butter to Peter.

"I look forward to working with you," Peter said, "but I want to know more about you first. I know you grew up around here, but were you born here?"

Hannah, who had taken a bite of bread, waited until she swallowed it and said, "Yeah. I was born and raised in Milwaukee. I spent my whole life here. I requested to be assigned here to be close to my mom, but part of me wishes I had requested a different location."

"Really? Why?"

"I guess I long for adventure. That's part of the reason I joined the FBI. I've been in Milwaukee for so long, I haven't experienced what life is like anywhere else."

"Have you not gone on any vacations?"

"Yeah, a few, but a vacation is not the same as living somewhere and experiencing the culture."

"I get that, but having a family is something I never knew. At least, it's something I don't remember. I would trade places with you in a second. Having someone you love who you can go to with a problem or just for the company seems priceless to me."

"You're right about that. I should learn to be more grateful for what I have."

"Tell me about your family," Peter said.

"Well, I'm an only child. My mom is a sales manager at a large hotel."

"What does a sales manager at a hotel sell?" Peter asked.

"You name it: weddings, tour groups, business meetings, sports teams, conventions, whatever."

"That sounds interesting. What about your dad?"

"I never knew my dad. He walked out on my mom before I was born."

"Oh, I'm sorry to hear that. That must have been hard on your mom."

"I'm sure it was, but you'd never know listening to her talk about him. Despite leaving her when she needed him the most,

Mom still thinks he's some kind of angel. It's not like he died in a war or something. He just left her."

"Maybe he did die," Peter offered. "Sometimes people who disappear do so because they're dead."

"No. I investigated public records and found nothing for anyone who fit his description and died at that time."

"Well, at least his daughter turned out well."

"Maybe not. I know it sounds sick for me to think this way, but I almost hope he is out there somewhere, buried in a shallow grave. At least that would excuse his behavior."

"I don't think it's unreasonable to feel that way. I don't remember anything before twenty-five years ago. I sometimes wonder why my parents never looked for me. If they had filed a missing person report when I lost my memory, we would have easily found each other, but they didn't. That makes me think they were either bad parents or died before that time. Honestly, I think if they were dead, I would feel better about them."

Hannah nodded. "It seems we have something in common. Let's talk about something less depressing. Tell me about yourself. Did any of those memories ever come back?"

"No. I'm afraid not."

"So, for all you know, you could have crash-landed here from another planet."

Peter smiled. "That is possible, although your yellow sun has not given me the power to leap tall buildings in a single bound."

Hannah laughed. "Maybe you need tights and a cape."

"I might be able to handle a cape, but I draw the line at tights."

"I'd like to see that," Hannah said, smiling. "But seriously, what do you think happened?"

"I have no idea. I woke up outside the church where you ran into me, which, by the way, was surprisingly hard."

"I needed it to be convincing," Hannah said.

"What about your shoulder? Did you really hurt it?"

"I did," she said, rubbing her shoulder. "I can still feel a little pain."

"Next time you want to fake meet someone, call out a random name and act like you know them. Then pretend you made a mistake. It's safer for everyone."

"I'll try to remember that next time," Hannah said. "Coincidentally, I did think I knew you when I first saw you."

"Really? From where?"

"I don't know. Living so close to you, perhaps we ran into each other once somewhere."

"Maybe. I'm not the best at paying attention. I would be a terrible witness if I ever saw a crime."

Hannah smiled. "So, tell me, what happened after you woke up near the church? How did you get your life in order?"

"When my life is in order, I'll let you know."

"Oh, it can't be that bad."

"I have good days and bad days. Having someone I can talk to helps make it a good day."

The waiter arrived with their food and set the plates on the table. "Bon Appétit," he said. "Is there anything else I can get you?"

Peter looked at Hannah, who shook her head. "No, thank you," he said.

Hannah swirled a few noodles onto her fork and put it in her mouth. "Mmmm, this is good."

Peter tasted his food and said, "I guess the waiter wasn't lying about how good this is."

"Did you have any doubts?"

"No, but if you can lie to me, maybe there are others like you."

"If there are, that waiter's not one of them." Hannah took another bite of her food. After she swallowed, she said, "What were we talking about?"

"My memory."

"Oh, yeah. What happened after you lost your memory and woke up near the church?"

"There was a young priest at the church, Father Azial. He took me in and let me spend the night. I think he assumed I was on drugs because I was confused and didn't know who I was. The next morning, I still had no memory of who I was or how I ended up in front of the church. It became clear I suffered from amnesia, but I had no head injury, so what happened has always been a mystery. The priest called me Peter, after his favorite Apostle."

"Is that the same priest you talked to this morning?"

"Yes. He said I needed to learn what God's intentions were for me. Maybe helping you is what God wants me to do."

"You've been seeing this priest for a long time. Is he not bothered by your ability?"

"No. I suppose priests don't lie much. He also seemed only mildly surprised when he learned people couldn't lie to me. He accepted it as a gift from God."

"How did you get the identity you have now?"

"Over the next year, the good father and a few social workers helped me find a job and housing. They also helped me get a legal identity and even set me up with therapists. Unfortunately, the jobs never lasted, and neither did the therapists."

"That must have been tough starting over like that."

"Yeah, it was, but I survived."

After dinner, Peter took Hannah home. He walked her up to the door and said goodnight, kissing her on the cheek. He knew their age difference made a relationship unlikely, and he was okay with that. He was happy to have someone he could talk to. "I enjoyed my time with you," he said.

"I did, too," Hannah said. "And that's the truth."

Chapter 3

Hannah picked up Peter at his house the following morning. She knocked on his door and waited. After a few seconds, the door opened. Peter smiled at Hannah and said, "I'm almost ready for my first day at work, Boss. Give me a minute. I need to get my coffee."

He returned thirty seconds later, holding a black travel mug.

Hannah looked him up and down. He wore a light blue, short-sleeved button-up shirt, tan chinos, and canvas boat shoes. "It's not exactly the look I expected, but we can work on it," she said.

Peter looked down at his clothing and asked, "What's wrong with how I'm dressed?"

"Nothing if you're going to a garden party."

"Well, I'm sorry. I don't exactly have a closet full of dress clothes."

"It's fine. We'll get you something."

Peter shook his head. "I'm not sure I want to look like one of you stuffed shirts."

Hannah looked at her outfit: a black blazer over a white shirt, black pants, and black, low-heeled shoes. "Do you think I'm a stuffed shirt?"

"Well, yes, but you stuff that shirt very nicely."

Hannah rolled her eyes. "We need to go."

When they walked to Hannah's car, Peter said, "A Ford Escape? Is this a government car?"

"No, it's my car. Why? Is there something wrong with it?"

"No. There's nothing wrong with it. I took you for someone more adventurous, like a Mustang girl."

"I'm more of an 'on a budget' kind of girl. I don't know what you've heard, but FBI agents aren't exactly raking in the cash, especially rookie agents."

"I see your point," Peter said.

When Peter got in the car, he placed his mug in a holder between the seats next to a similar mug. "I see you're a coffee drinker, too," he said.

"I've never been a morning person," Hannah said. "I need the caffeine."

"I find coffee to be relaxing."

"Seriously? You must be wired backward."

Peter smiled and looked around the car. He popped open the glove box. There was nothing in it except the car's manual. He closed it and looked in the side pocket.

"What are you looking for?" Hannah asked.

"I'm looking for trash. This car is immaculate. Did you just buy it?"

"No. I've had it for a while."

"Did you clean it before picking me up?"

"No, I didn't. Why does this surprise you? Your car was clean when you picked me up last night."

"It was clean because I cleaned it before I picked you up."

"Well, I'm not a pig. I like a clean car, so I don't let trash accumulate."

"It's not only trash. You must keep a towel and a bottle of Armor All in your car."

"What kind of person do you think I am?" Hannah asked as she reached under her seat and pulled out a container of disposable Armor All wipes. "These work much better."

Peter smiled and shook his head. "Of course."

They drove to the FBI field office south of the city. Peter followed Hannah through security and up to the second floor. They exited the elevator into a large room with offices around much of the perimeter and many cubicles in the center. They could see Lake Michigan through the large windows at the far end.

Hannah led Peter through the maze of cubicles and stopped at her desk. Her area was spotless, with nothing unnecessary taking up space. No photos of family or friends. No potted plants. No souvenirs. No pieces of paper with notes written on them.

"You must have Armor All wipes in your office, too."

"Don't be silly," Hannah said. She opened her top drawer and took out a container of Lysol wipes.

Peter laughed. "You are too much."

Hannah sat at her desk and checked her emails. Seeing nothing critical, she stood up and said, "Let's see if Tim and Ben are here yet."

They found them in a conference room. Ben shook Peter's hand and said, "It's good to see you again." He looked Hannah up and down, smiled, and said, "Good morning, Hannah."

Peter noticed the look but said nothing.

After everyone exchanged greetings, Tim said, "We're glad you decided to help, Peter. I must say that I'm a little concerned about you two taking the lead on this. I'm sure Hannah is a fine agent, but she doesn't have enough experience, and you have no experience. It could be dangerous for you."

"Are you concerned for us, or are you worried about your ego?" Peter asked.

"I think a little of both," Tim said.

"Would you like to reconsider your position?"

"Well, now that you mention it, taking a backseat might be better under the circumstances."

"I thought you would see it that way," Peter said.

"Let's get to work," Hannah said.

Inside the room was a long table with eight chairs. A large monitor hung from the wall at the far end. Hannah and Peter sat beside each other at the end, near the screen, and across from Ben, who had his laptop on the table.

Tim stood near the television with a remote control in his hand. When he pressed a button, a photo appeared on the screen. Two men, one middle-aged and the other in his late twenties, stood outside somewhere. The photo appeared to have been taken with a telephoto lens. The blurred background made it difficult to determine their location.

The taller of the two, the man on the left, had a full mustache and wore a beige suit that matched his beige Panama hat, which had a black band around it. A cigar dangled from the man's right hand.

The man on the right dressed more casually than his boss. He was clean-shaven and wore aviator sunglasses but no hat. His dark hair was slightly disheveled, suggesting that someone had taken the photo on a breezy day. He appeared to be listening intently to the other man.

Tim pointed at the man on the left. "This is Salvador Salinas. He is the head of the El Círculo de Confianza, which is one of the most powerful drug cartels in Mexico. The man next to him is his right-hand man, Diego Ortiz. We have reports that Ortiz was in Milwaukee a little over a month ago, but we can't confirm that."

"I thought you guys monitored people like that with facial recognition software," Peter said.

"It's not as widespread as you think," Ben said. "Plus, this is the only photo we have of Diego Ortiz, and there's not enough detail for a good match."

"We can confirm that the number of fentanyl deaths has spiked over the last couple of weeks," Tim continued. "We think Ortiz has established a trafficking route from Mexico to Milwaukee."

"Why Milwaukee?" Peter asked.

"That is something we need to figure out," Tim said.

"We think they chose Milwaukee for a specific reason," Ben said.

"What would that be?" Peter asked.

"We don't know yet, but Milwaukee is not geographically ideal. Chicago would be a better choice if you wanted to distribute your drugs across the Midwest."

"Maybe that's why they chose Milwaukee," Hannah suggested. "I mean, who would suspect it?"

"Apparently, you guys would," Peter said. "From what you tell me, it was obvious from the start. Someone leaked that Ortiz was in Milwaukee, and now you are dealing with more fentanyl deaths than ever. These people either suck at keeping secrets, or they don't care if you know."

"Peter has a point," Hannah said. "What if they don't care? What if they want us to believe their base of operations is here, but it's actually in Fond du Lac or Kenosha, or who knows where?"

"That's what we are here to find out," Tim said.

"So where do we start?" Peter asked.

Tim reached into his pocket and pulled out a watch. He handed it to Peter and said, "You can start by putting this on."

Peter looked at the watch and said, "I don't wear a watch."

He tried returning it, but Tim raised his hand and said, "I don't care if you don't wear a watch. You need to wear this one. We were gracious enough to take a backseat on this operation. The least you can do is cooperate a little. This watch will help us know your location at all times. It also has all our numbers programmed in, so you can use it to call us if you need to. Best of all, it has a panic button. Hold the red button down for two seconds, and we'll know you're in trouble."

"Okay, fine," Peter said, putting the watch on his wrist. "I'm not crazy about you knowing where I am all the time, but I can see how it could be helpful."

"Absolutely," Tim said. "You don't have the training we have, so this will help keep you safe."

Peter looked at Hannah and said, "So, what should we do first?"

"I have an idea." She turned to Ben and asked, "Can you find someone local who survived a recent fentanyl overdose?"

"Of course," Ben said. He opened his laptop and started searching. After a few minutes, he said, "I see one at a hospital nearby. I'll send the information to your phone."

A few seconds later, Hannah's phone beeped. She looked at it and said, "I got it. Thanks."

***

Hannah led Peter to the parking lot, where they picked up a black Chevy Impala. "It's a good thing we're not undercover," Peter said as they got in. "They might as well print 'Government Vehicle' on the back."

"If we were undercover, I would let you drive your car."

"That might be fun. We could be like Miami Vice."

"Who?"

"Never mind."

It took ten minutes to drive to the hospital. Once inside, they approached the help desk and asked the young woman behind the counter where they could find George Roberts. She tapped a few keys and looked at her computer screen. "He's in room 315 on the third floor."

When they reached his room, they found the door open, so Hannah knocked three times and walked in, followed by Peter. The harsh overhead lighting and the smell of bleach made the room feel cold and unwelcoming.

Peter thought hospitals might be like restaurants where the chairs are deliberately uncomfortable enough to ensure no one lingers too long after their meal but not too uncomfortable to discourage people from returning. Perhaps the atmosphere in a hospital motivates patients to want to recover.

The room had two beds, but the bed near the window was empty. In the other bed lay a man of around thirty-five. He was thin and pale, with beads of sweat clinging to his skin. He had dark, stringy hair and dark circles under his eyes. "Are you with the hospital?" he asked in a slow, raspy voice.

Hannah took out her ID and held it up. "I'm Agent Hannah Meyers with the FBI. This is Peter Beckett. We want to ask you a few questions, Mr. Roberts."

"You don't look like an FBI agent," Roberts said to Peter.

"Thank you for noticing," Peter said.

"He's a special advisor," Hannah said.

"So, why would the FBI care about me?" Roberts asked. "I didn't break any federal laws."

"Yes, you did," Hannah said. "Possession of a controlled substance, like fentanyl, is a federal crime."

"Don't you have more important people to harass? Besides, you can't prove that. I wasn't in possession of fentanyl or any other drugs."

"It was on your toxicology report. Having it inside your body is still considered possession."

Roberts sighed, ran his fingers through his hair, and looked out the window briefly. He looked back and said, "Okay, fine. I admit I took it, but I didn't know it was fentanyl. I thought I was taking OxyContin."

"OxyContin is still illegal without a prescription," Hannah said. "Do you have a prescription for it?"

Roberts slowly shook his head and nervously played with his fingernails. "No, but I did at one time. Listen, I'm just a guy with a problem. I used to be a roofer, but I fell off a roof and hurt my back. I need something for the pain. Give me a break, will ya? The FBI must have bigger fish to fry."

"You are right, Mr. Roberts, and you are going to help us find those bigger fish," Hannah said. "Who did you buy the drugs from?"

"I don't know. I never saw him before."

"What did he look like?"

"I wasn't paying attention. I didn't expect I would need to identify him later."

"You're in a lot of trouble, Mr. Roberts. Things could go much smoother for you if you cooperate."

After a long pause, he said, "Okay, but you didn't hear it from me. The man was Hispanic, about twenty-five years old, with a thin Mustache. He talked with an accent."

"Where did you meet him?" Hannah asked.

"At a convenience store on 17th and Walnut."

Hannah thought momentarily and said, "There's no convenience store there."

"It was on Walnut somewhere. I don't remember exactly where."

"Who told you to go there?"

Roberts hesitated and said, "I don't remember."

"Seriously?"

Roberts slowly shook his head. "I guess I haven't been thinking clearly since my accident."

Hannah looked at Peter and said, "You can step in any time now."

Peter smiled, "I was enjoying watching you work."

"Well, it's your turn. We're not paying you to watch me work."

"Okay, if you insist." Peter stepped closer and said, "Mr. Roberts, please tell us the truth. Let's start with the drug dealer. Where did you meet him?"

Roberts hesitated and said, "I met him where I told you, on 17th and Walnut."

"You met him on the street corner?"

"Not exactly. I got on the bus there. Someone told me to sit in the back of the bus, which I did."

"Was the drug dealer sitting in the back of the bus?" Peter asked.

"Yes, he was."

"What did he look like?"

"He was white. About twenty-five. He was clean-shaven with fairly long, sandy-blonde hair."

"Did he tell you his name?"

"No, of course not. And I didn't ask."

"Who was the guy who told you about the dealer? Peter asked.

Roberts' mouth opened, but nothing came out for a couple of seconds. Then he said, "His name is John Martin."

"Okay, now we're getting somewhere. How do you know John Martin?"

"He's an employee where I used to work."

"Where did you used to work?"

"The place is called Bishop Brothers Roofing."

"Do you know where John Martin lives?"

"No. I've never been to his house."

"Is there anything else I should know?" Peter asked.

Roberts shook his head. "No. That's all I know. I swear."

"I believe you," Peter said. He looked at Hannah. "Do you believe him?"

"We believe you, Mr. Roberts. We appreciate your honesty. You need not worry about the FBI any longer."

When they left the room, Peter said, "It's Sunday. That roofing company is probably closed."

"Good point," Hannah said. She took her phone out and called Ben. She asked for the address of John Martin, who works for Bishop Brothers Roofing.

Chapter 4

Hannah's phone beeped after they returned to the car. Ben had already found John Martin's address and forwarded it to her. She held up her phone and said, "We have our next stop. He's about ten minutes from here."

They found the address Ben had given them a few miles southwest of the hospital. It was a two-story home in an old part of town. The house had tan vinyl siding, but the porch was white, and much of the paint was peeling off. Next door, a man mowed his lawn.

Hannah rang the bell, and they waited. A tall, muscular man in his mid-twenties answered the door.

"Are you John Martin?" Hannah asked, raising her voice to be heard over the noise of the lawn mower.

"Yes. What's this about?"

Hannah showed her ID to him and asked, "Can you come outside so we can talk to you?"

The man stiffened, and his grip on the door handle tightened. What is this about?"

"Please, come outside."

Martin stepped outside and closed the door behind him. A strong breeze blew his blonde, shoulder-length hair in front of his face. He pulled his hair behind his ear and said, "How can I help you?"

"We need to talk to you about George Roberts," Hannah said.

Martin looked away and then back at Hannah. "What about him?"

The sound of the lawn mower stopped, giving Hannah's voice a break. "He said you arranged a meeting between him and a drug dealer."

Martin's eyes widened. "What? That lying son of a bitch! I haven't even seen George for months. He must have been high again."

Hannah looked at Peter. "Can we not go through this again?"

Peter smiled at Hannah and then looked at Martin. "Mr. Martin. Who is this drug dealer, and where can we find him?"

Martin hesitated and then said, "His name is Bob McMurry. I went to high school with him. I don't know his address."

"You have his phone number, correct?" Peter asked.

"Yes, I do."

"What is his phone number?"

Martin took out his phone, found the contact, and showed it to Peter and Hannah.

Hannah copied the number onto her small notebook and put it back in her pocket.

Peter took out his phone, started a video recording, and said, "Okay, Mr. Martin. This is for the record. What do you get out of referring people to your drug dealer friend?"

Martin hesitated again. He appeared to resist the temptation to answer, but his resistance quickly vanished. "He gives me twenty percent for new customers and ten percent for repeat orders."

Peter put his phone away and said, "It ends now. Is that clear?"

"Yes. Very clear."

When they returned to the car, Hannah said, "That was quite charitable. You didn't think we should have him arrested?"

"Did you want to waste time with him?"

"No, but I was surprised we are on the same page."

"Perhaps we are not so different."

Hannah took out her phone and dialed a number. After a few seconds, she said, "Ben, we need another address. This one is for Bob or Robert McMurry. He's a possible dealer. I'll text you his phone number."

After sending the text, she put her phone away and said, "I'm getting hungry. Let's have lunch."

"Sounds good to me."

***

Hannah drove to a nearby restaurant. Peter looked surprised. "A burger joint? I figured you for a health nut."

"You obviously don't know me as much as I don't know you."

They went inside, placed their order, and then sat at one of the tables to wait for their food.

"Why would you assume I'm a health nut?" Hannah asked.

"Because you're so fit and trim."

"I try to eat healthy, but I like to eat something that tastes good now and then. I also work out almost every day, so I don't feel guilty about it. What about you? You're in good shape. Are you a health nut?"

"No, I guess I am a lot like you. I don't work out at the gym, but I have a bike that I ride a lot when the weather is good."

"Really? Do you wear those funny clothes and ride in groups?"

"Seriously? Do you think I'm a social butterfly?"

"Sorry. I wasn't thinking."

A man arrived with their food and set it on the table. Peter looked at his hamburger and said, "This thing is huge."

"I've never finished one yet."

"Do you come here often?"

"Only when I'm in the mood for a good hamburger."

Hannah's phone beeped. She looked at it and said, "It's a message from Ben. He sent us an address."

She texted him back that they would be heading there shortly.

When they finished eating and got up to leave, four teenage boys walked in, all around thirteen or fourteen. The biggest one spotted two other boys sitting at a table. They were around the same age. They likely attended school together. The boys at the table were skinny. One wore glasses. The big boy walked over to the other boys, followed by his entourage. He said, "Well, well, well, if it isn't Dork One and Dork Two. Did your mommies let you come here alone?"

The big boy knocked a chocolate shake over onto the lap of the boy with glasses. "Oops," he said.

The boy with glasses quickly stood up. It looked like he wanted to punch the big boy, who pulled his arm back, preparing to punch first. Peter grabbed the kid's arm and said, "Stop!"

The boy put his arm down and turned to look at Peter. "We're just joking around," he said.

"Here's a joke for you," Peter said. "Tell me, what is the most embarrassing thing about you? Tell me something you don't want anyone to know."

The kid looked around and back at Peter, "I wet my bed until I was eight."

The other kids started laughing, including the two nerdy kids. Hannah showed her ID and said, "FBI! You kids need to leave."

All four boys looked surprised, but none of them moved.

"Now!" Hannah yelled.

The boys nearly tripped over each other as they scrambled out the door.

"I didn't know you could be so authoritative," Peter said.

"You surprised me, too," Hannah said. "I've never seen karma bite a bully in the ass quite like that before."

"I've learned everyone has an Achilles heel."

"Oh, yeah? What's mine."

"You, I haven't figured out yet. I'm not sure I want to. I like the mystery."

"If you had to guess, what do you think would be my weakness?"

Peter thought momentarily and said, "I don't think you have a weakness."

"Now you are lying."

"I thought you sucked at detecting lies."

"Some are just too obvious. So tell me what you think."

"You don't want to know what I think."

"C'mon, tell me. People have been telling you the truth your whole life. It's time you return the favor."

After a long pause, Peter said, "Okay, but remember, you asked. I think you need recognition. You need someone to be proud of you. Not just anyone. You need a man to be proud of you."

Hannah stared at Peter for several seconds and finally said, "That's crazy. You just made that up to ruffle my feathers."

"Are your feathers ruffled?"

Hannah looked at her watch. "We need to get going."

***

They arrived at the address Ben gave them and parked on the street. It was an old, brick, three-story apartment building. McMurry's apartment was on the first floor. They walked through the main double doors. The apartment they were looking for was the second door on the left. Hannah knocked, and they waited. After thirty seconds, the door finally opened a crack. A chain lock prevented it from opening further. Part of a face appeared.

Hannah showed her ID and said, "Mr. McMurry, we need you to open the door."

McMurry closed the door but locked it rather than releasing the chain. When they heard the door lock, Hannah realized what was happening and tried the door handle. "Wait here," she said to Peter. "Hold the door. Don't let him out."

She ran out the front door and around the building to the back. She didn't see anyone, but she did see an open window. She looked inside. It was near the dining room. She saw a couple of small cardboard boxes on the dining room table with several pill bottles next to the boxes.

She climbed through the window. Once inside, she took out her gun. She couldn't be sure that McMurry climbed out of the window. He might have opened it so they would think he escaped.

She stood between the kitchen and the dining room. She looked around. The place was messy but not dirty. Both of the boxes on the dining room table were open. She looked inside the nearest one. It was half-filled with pills. The other box contained empty prescription bottles with no labels. Several of the bottles on the table near the boxes had pills in them.

She searched the small apartment, looking for McMurry. When convinced it was safe, she tried to open the door for Peter, but he held it closed.

"It's okay," she said. "It's me."

Peter let go, and Hannah opened the door. Walking inside, he said, "I take it he got away."

"Yeah, but now we know who the dealer is."

"What do we do now?"

Hannah took out her phone. "We get help."

She called Tim and told him the situation. He told her he would contact the local police and have a BOLO put out for the man. She also asked him to get a warrant so they could thoroughly search the apartment.

As they waited, Peter noticed a small, framed photo on an end table. It was a picture of McMurry, with short hair, standing next to a young woman. Considering the current length of his hair, the photo was at least a year old.

He held up the photo and said, "This might help find the guy."

"That will work," she said. She took out her phone and took a photo of it. She wasn't sure who to send it to, so she sent it to both Tim and Ben. Ben was the computer expert, but Tim was the leader and would get the warrant.

It took a while, but eventually, several Milwaukee police officers showed up with a warrant. Everyone did a thorough search of the apartment. They found a ledger with transactions of over ten thousand dollars. Numbers represented customers, and initials represented people owed a commission. They found nothing to indicate where the drugs were coming from.

When they finished, they drove back to the FBI building and reviewed their day with Tim and Bill. Hannah then drove Peter home. "I'll pick you up at eight tomorrow," she said as he got out of her car. "Is that too early for you?"

"No. Eight is fine. I'll see you then."

***

Hannah didn't go straight home. She drove to her mother's house, less than a mile from where she lived. Her mother lived in a nice, middle-class neighborhood. Her home sat on a corner lot, with the front of the house facing one street and the attached two-car garage facing the adjoining street. A white picket fence enclosed the front yard.

Hannah parked in the driveway and got out of the car. She looked at the house for a moment. She had many good memories there as a child. She walked up the steps and knocked on the door.

The door opened ten seconds later. Her mom, with a surprised look on her face, said, "Oh, Honey. I didn't expect you. Come on in."

"Hi, Mom," Hannah said as she walked inside.

"This is your home, too. You don't have to knock."

"I know, but I wanted to make sure you weren't with a man or something."

Her mom laughed. "Oh, Honey. You know there's only one man for me."

"He's been gone my whole life, Mom. It's time you started thinking about your happiness."

"It's your happiness I worry about, Dear. When was the last time you had a serious relationship?"

"We're talking about you, Mom. I've had many more relationships than you have."

"You only meet your soulmate once, Hannah. I met mine, your father. It's your turn."

"You are impossible, Mom."

Hannah's mom looked at her for a moment. "What's wrong, Hannah? Why are you here?"

"Why do you think something's wrong? Can't I visit you because I like to see you?"

"Of course you can, but usually, something is bothering you when you show up unannounced."

Hannah was at a loss for words.

"Come. Sit down," her mom said, leading her to the living room. Hannah sat on the sofa while her mom sat next to her on a chair. "Now, tell me what's bothering you."

Hannah shook her head. "Nothing. I'm fine."

"You don't look fine."

After a long pause, Hannah said, "I just started working with this man."

"Really? Are you attracted to him?"

"What? No. It's not like that. He's twenty years older than I am. Maybe more."

"Okay, so what's the problem?"

"He said something to me today that bothered me a little. He thought I needed a man to be proud of me."

"That sounds kind of sexist," her mom said.

"I don't think he meant it that way."

"If he didn't mean it that way, why are you upset?"

"I'm upset because I'm not sure he's wrong."

"Really? You think you need a man to be proud of you?"

"I don't know. Let me put it this way. Almost my whole life, I felt I needed to prove that I could do anything a man could do. I think I've proven that to some degree, but it feels unsatisfying."

"You have accomplished so much. I'm so proud of you. You should be proud of yourself."

"I know you're proud of me, Mom, and I appreciate it, but you would be proud of me no matter what I accomplished. If I were a nurse or even a stay-at-home mom, you would still be proud of me."

"Of course. Both of those jobs are hard."

"That's not what I mean, Mom."

"I get it, Hannah. You think I'm too easily impressed, so being proud of you doesn't hold as much weight."

"That makes me sound unappreciative, and that's not the case," Hannah said.

Hannah's mom sighed. "I'm sorry, Honey. Growing up without a father must have been hard on you. I didn't think about it when you were young, but I guess there were things you needed that I couldn't give you."

"It's fine, Mom. You did the best you could."

"So, do you think you have a desire to impress this new man?"

"That's exactly it. Why should I care what he thinks?"

"Well, he is your elder. Maybe he's the closest thing you have to a father figure."

"I don't know. Maybe. I just know I don't like feeling like I have to impress someone who isn't my boss. I also don't like that he seems to know me better than I know him."

"You know what they say, Hannah. With age comes wisdom."

"I suppose that would explain it."

"Why don't you stay for dinner? I have a shepherd's pie in the oven."

"That sounds good, Mom. I'd love to stay."

Chapter 5

The following morning, Hannah and Peter met Tim and Ben at the FBI office. Tim informed them that the police had caught the drug dealer, McMurry, and handed Hannah a piece of paper. "That's the address to the precinct where they're holding him. They say he's not talking."

"I think we can fix that," Hannah said, looking at Peter.

Peter smiled. "This should be fun."

They drove to the address Tim had given them and parked on the street near the police station. They walked inside and approached an officer behind a counter. He was a tall, muscular man who seemed out of place behind a reception counter.

"Good morning. What can I do for you?" the officer asked.

Hannah showed him her identification and said, "We'd like to speak with your captain."

He picked up his phone and dialed a number. After a few seconds, he said, "A couple of people from the FBI are here to see you." When he hung up the phone, he got up, opened the door, and invited Hannah and Peter to follow him.

He led them through a large open room with numerous desks. Most were empty. The room smelled of stale coffee, and a constant buzz emanated from some of the fluorescent lights. They reached a room with glass windows. The door read, "Captain Gabriel Garcia." The officer knocked and opened the door, motioning for Hannah and Peter to enter.

As they entered, the captain stood and walked around his desk to greet them. He was a handsome man in his mid-forties, a little taller than average. "I'm Gabe Garcia," he said. "I was expecting you."

They shook hands, and Hannah said, "I'm Special Agent Hannah Meyers, and this is Peter Beckett. He is an interrogation specialist working with us on this case."

"Interrogation specialist? I hope you are not talking about torture?"

"Oh, no," Hannah said. "His methods are non-violent and much more effective."

"This I have to see," Garcia said. He picked up his phone, dialed a number, and said, "We need McMurry in Interrogation Room One."

"Come with me," Garcia said. He led them to a small room with a large window. In the center of the room stood a video camera on a tripod. On the other side of the window was a desk with a chair on each side. Two officers led the man Hannah and Peter had seen the day before into the room. They made him sit down in one of the chairs and then handcuffed him to the desk. When the officers left the room, Garcia said, "Okay, let's see what you got."

Peter opened the door to the interrogation room and motioned for Hannah to go first. He then stepped in behind her. Hannah said, "Remember us?"

"I've got nothing to say to you. The only person I want to talk to is my lawyer."

"You are under no obligation to speak with us without your lawyer," Hannah said. "Do you understand?"

McMurry, obviously confused by Hannah's statement, slowly nodded.

"We need you to tell us you understand you don't have to talk to us," Hannah said.

"Okay. I understand."

Hannah turned to Peter and motioned for him to take the lead.

Peter stepped forward and said, "Mr. McMurry. Do you confess that you were selling illegal narcotics?"

McMurry's mouth opened, but nothing came out for several seconds. Finally, he said, "Yes. I confess. I've been selling illegal narcotics."

"Who do you get your narcotics from?"

"I don't know. There is an arranged drop-off and pick-up point. I never see anyone."

"Where is that?" Peter asked.

Hannah took out her notebook and started taking notes.

"I don't know the address, but it's on Chicago Street. It's called Third Ward Fitness."

"So, how do you make the exchange?"

"There is a particular locker at the gym. Every Monday before four, I open it and put cash in it for my next order. I then pick up my order after ten on Tuesday."

"Which locker is it?"

"It changes every week."

"How do you know which one to open?"

"I look for the red Master lock."

"Do you have a key, or is it a combination lock?"

"It's a combination lock."

"What's the combination?" Peter asked.

"It's seventeen, twenty-four, twelve."

Hannah touched Peter's arm. When he looked at her, she said, "Ask him how much he puts in the locker."

"How much money do you put in the locker?"

"It depends on what I need," McMurry said. "Last week, it was a thousand dollars."

"One more question," Peter said. "How did you get recruited into this operation?"

"I was dealing weed about three months ago. A man approached me and said I could make a lot more money selling pills."

"What did this man look like?"

"I don't remember exactly. I only saw him that one time. He was white and maybe in his thirties. He was well-groomed. He had short, dark brown hair and a beard. He also wore a suit and tie."

"Not exactly your typical drug dealer," Hannah said. "I think we have enough. Thanks so much for your cooperation. We'll be sure to tell everyone how helpful you were."

"Wait! You can't do that!" he yelled as Hannah and Peter left the room. "They'll kill me!"

They met Captain Garcia on the other side of the door. He said, "Wow! I can't believe you got him to spill everything so easily."

"Peter has a special gift," Hannah said.

There was a flash of recognition on Garcia's face. "Oh, I see. I wish we had someone like you working in this department."

Hannah handed Garcia a business card. "Please, give me a call if you learn anything more about this drug operation."

When Hannah and Peter got in the car to leave, Hannah said, "Captain Garcia didn't seem very surprised about your abilities."

"I noticed that too," Peter said. "It's like he met someone like me before."

"I told you about the list of special people the FBI has. Since meeting you, I'm starting to believe that there may be many other people out there with unusual abilities. Maybe Garcia has met one of those special people."

"I guess that's possible," Peter said. "It's also possible he's just a man who is hard to impress."

***

They returned to the FBI headquarters and met Tim and Ben in the conference room. They sat at the table and discussed what they had learned from McMurry.

"Today is Monday," Hannah said. "We need to put cash in that locker and watch who takes it."

"I don't know how quickly we can get the cash," Tim said.

"Seriously?" Peter said. "The way the government spends money getting a thousand dollars should be a piece of cake."

"I wish it were that easy, but you know the government. There's always a certain amount of red tape we must go through," Tim said.

"You know what? You don't need money," Peter said. "Just set up a spy camera and see who opens the locker. Maybe you can open and close it in case there's a sensor on it."

Ben nodded. "I think that will work. I can go in there and set it up."

"I suppose I should probably mention that what we are planning to do is illegal," Peter said.

"We know," Tim said, "but we don't plan on using the video in court. We only need to find the next link in the chain."

"Well, if you're okay with it, so am I," Peter said.

"Okay, then, it's settled," Tim said. "While Ben is getting everything he needs ready, I'll investigate who owns the gym. The owner may be involved or unaware of what's happening."

"What should we do?" Hannah asked.

"Maybe you two can find out if someone monitors who comes and goes at that fitness center. Also, make sure there are no cameras in the locker room."

"Will do," Hannah said as she stood. She left the conference room, followed by Peter.

***

Third Ward Fitness occupied the left half of the bottom floor of an old, five-story brick building. The top four floors were apartments. Hannah parked in the only available spot near the gym, and they went inside. The air smelled of sweat and rubber. The sounds of weights clanking and the hum of treadmills filled the room.

A few steps inside the door, a young woman sat behind a desk. Behind her, to the left, were a dozen or so weight machines near the windows. To the right was an area devoted to free weights. Along the back wall were several treadmills and exercise bikes. The back right corner had a door that was probably an office. The wall to the right had two doors, one leading to the men's locker room and the other to the women's locker room. About fifteen people were inside working out. The woman at the desk looked up, smiled, and said, "Good morning. Can I help you?"

"Good morning," Hannah said. "We're thinking about joining a gym. Do you have time to give us a tour?"

"It would be my pleasure," the woman said. "May I ask how you heard about us?"

"An acquaintance of ours, Robert McMurry, said we should check it out," Hannah said.

"Bobby? That was sweet of him. I'll have to thank him next time he's in."

"Do you know Bobby personally?" Peter asked.

"No, not really. I only know him from here. He's a bit of a flirt, and he's cute. If I didn't have a boyfriend, I would definitely let him have his way with me."

The woman cleared her throat and stood up. "I'm sorry. I don't know why I said that. Let me show you around."

She led them to the group of weight machines and said, "These are our weight machines. Each one targets a different muscle group. These are beneficial for anyone but especially helpful for people who are out of shape or new to working out. They're easily adjustable. You just set the weight to whatever is comfortable for you."

"I'm curious," Peter said. "What does Bobby do for a living?"

"I don't know," the woman said. "I thought he was a friend of yours."

"No, just an acquaintance. He told me once what he did, but I don't remember. When I see him, I'll be embarrassed to tell him I forgot."

"Sorry, but I can't help you there."

"Do you own this place?" Peter asked.

"Oh, no," the woman said. "I just work here. The owner is in the back doing paperwork."

"Does he know Bobby?"

"I doubt it. I've never seen him speak to Bobby."

The woman continued with the tour. Hannah and Peter scanned the ceiling and walls for mounted cameras. They also kept their eyes open for less obvious places where cameras might be hidden. They found none.

When the woman finished the tour, Hannah asked, "Can we see the locker rooms?"

"Of course," she said and pointed to the doors. "They're right over there. I'll meet you at the front desk when you're ready."

Peter went into the men's locker room. To the left was a row of sinks. To the right were two long benches, each with lockers on either side. Past the lockers along the opposite wall were several shower stalls. Peter looked around for hidden cameras. Seeing none, he looked for the red Master lock. He found it in the middle of the first row of lockers. He also saw other colors of Master locks on random lockers. In addition to the red, there were blue, green, and purple. There was also a silver lock with a red dial. He thought each lock might be for a different drug dealer, or there was a sale on colorful locks recently.

Peter met Hannah outside the locker room. They told the woman they would be back and left before she could get them to commit to signing a contract. Once they got into the car, they compared notes.

"I saw the red lock plus several other colors," Peter said. "This might be a hub for drug dealers."

"I wonder if there are more places like this," Hannah said.

"I don't know. There could be," Peter said. "What did you find in your locker room?"

"Not much. A few plain locks. Nothing colorful."

"These people must be sexist," Peter said. "They only hire male drug dealers."

"Maybe men are the only ones stupid enough to get involved in something that can ruin their lives."

Peter looked at Hannah. "Are you dissing on men?"

"No, but you have to wonder why you never see women drug dealers."

"You never see women bricklayers either. That doesn't mean men are stupid."

"I'm not saying all men are stupid. Just the stupid ones."

"Well, I'm glad you cleared that up."

Chapter 6

Agent Ben Green had changed out of his suit and into workout clothing. He wore black shorts and a gray T-shirt that was tight on him. He was a muscular man who was no stranger to the gym. He carried a gym bag with him into Third Ward Fitness. The young woman behind the counter smiled when he approached.

Ben smiled back and said, "Hi. I'm visiting here from Virginia. My hotel doesn't have a workout center, so I want to see if I can work out here. I'd be happy to pay whatever your daily rate is."

"Of course," she said, smiling again. "It will be ten dollars for today, or I can get you a week pass for thirty dollars."

"Today will be fine," Ben said. "I'll be heading home in a couple of days."

After he gave the woman ten dollars and signed in, he went to the free weight area and started his workout. He wanted his reason for being there to look legitimate, but he was also telling the truth. His hotel didn't have a workout center, except for treadmills, which he didn't care for. This was his opportunity to maintain his workout routine, at least somewhat. A large television hung on the wall, showing the news. The volume was muted, but the screen displayed captions at the bottom.

Ben watched during his sets. A reporter interviewed a middle-aged woman with a dark complexion and long black hair. "We are here with Alderwoman Sofia Russo, who has started a recall campaign to remove Mayor Monroe from office," the reporter said. "Can you tell us why you feel that such a drastic step is necessary?"

"Of course. There are several reasons, including the mayor's unfriendly attitude towards business, which has resulted in a loss of millions of dollars in potential tax revenue. What bothers me the most is the reports I've been hearing about Mexican drug cartels bringing their drugs directly to Milwaukee. Mayor Monroe's soft stance on crime has allowed this to happen. In just these last few weeks, fentanyl overdoses have skyrocketed, and the problem will only get worse unless we get a mayor in here who will be tough on crime, especially drug trafficking."

The mention of fentanyl sparked Ben's interest, and he decided to wait until the story finished before resuming his workout. He wiped the sweat from his forehead and stepped closer to the television.

"Are you accusing the mayor of being complacent in the illegal drug trade?"

"Those are your words, not mine, but I have to wonder why he is doing almost nothing to stop it."

"Thank you for speaking with us today, Alderwoman Russo," the reporter said. He turned to the camera. "This is Kevin Reed for Channel 23 News. Now back to the studio."

A woman appeared on the screen and said, "In other news, Mayor Monroe continues to voice his opposition to the South Shore redevelopment plan."

Ben looked away from the television and resumed his workout. When he finished, he went into the locker room. Two men stood near the sinks, having a conversation. He looked for the red Master lock. When he saw it, he removed a towel from his bag, placed the bag in the locker across from the red Master lock, and then secured his locker with a padlock. He then showered.

When he finished showering, the locker room was empty. He quickly dried, removed his bag, and put his clothes on. He removed a small wireless camera from his bag. He had rigged it so it would stick to the inside of a locker magnetically.

Using his phone as a video monitor, he adjusted the camera until it was over one of the built-in slits designed for airflow.

Suddenly, he heard the locker room door creak open. He quickly closed his locker as a man walked past him. The man continued to the next row of lockers. Ben heard the sound of a locker opening and relaxed. He rechecked the video. Luckily, he positioned it perfectly the first time. The top and bottom of the frame were obstructed slightly, but there was sufficient coverage to see whoever opened the red lock.

He placed his lock back on the locker and then used the combination Hannah gave him to open the red lock. The locker was empty, and Ben saw no device that would indicate whether someone had opened the lock. He put the lock back on and left the gym, returning to his hotel to change back into his work clothes.

***

Hannah and Peter went out for lunch and returned to the office when Ben returned. They all met in the conference room. Ben showed them the video feed from the camera. He said it had a motion sensor and would record anyone accessing the locker.

"What about the Gym owner?" Hannah asked. "Did you learn anything about him?"

"Yes. He seems clean," Tim said. "I couldn't find any link to drugs or any other illegal behavior. Of course, that doesn't prove he's innocent."

"We spoke with an employee there," Hannah said. "She had no idea what McMurry did for work, and she never saw the boss talk to him."

"He probably has no idea what goes on in his gym," Ben said.

"What should we do now?" Peter asked.

"There's not much you can do at the moment," Tim said. "Why don't you guys take a break and meet us in front of the gym before four? If McMurry is right, we should know something soon after."

After Hannah and Peter left the conference room, Hannah said, "You saw my place. Why don't you show me yours?"

"There isn't much to see," Peter said.

"Humor me."

"Okay. My cat missed lunch today, so he will be happy to see us."

"Oh, you're a cat person, huh?"

"I like cats and dogs. They're both good company. Better than people."

"I can't argue with you, but we all need human companionship."

"That is exactly why this so-called gift of mine is a curse."

"I get it, Peter. When this case is over, I will gladly hang out with you. Perhaps we can determine what makes me unique. Maybe other people are like me."

"That would be nice."

When they arrived at Peter's house, he unlocked the door and went inside. He held the door open for Hannah and then closed it behind her. Sammy, the cat, bypassed Peter and rubbed his face on Hannah's legs.

"It seems you are Sammy-approved," Peter said.

Hannah stooped down and petted Sammy, who rubbed his face against her hand. She then followed Peter into the living room.

Her mouth hung open in awe as she looked around. The polished hardwood floors reflected the light from the window. One wall was lined with built-in bookshelves, partially filled with old books and small, hand-carved wooden figurines, each shaped into an animal or a tree.

Everything was unique. The sofa and chairs were crafted from solid wood, featuring curved armrests and thick cushions. A hand-carved mantel framed the fireplace. It depicted an underwater scene with fish, turtles, whales, and even a mermaid.

A floor lamp stood on each side of the room. Thick, natural branches, polished to a shine, held large, wicker lampshades.

"This room is amazing," Hannah said. "Did you make all of this?"

Peter nodded. "I have a lot of time on my hands."

"Everything is so beautiful. The next time I need furniture, I know where to come."

"On a rookie's salary? I doubt you can afford me," Peter said, laughing. "It's too bad because your home really needs something."

Hannah smiled and playfully slapped Peter's arm. "Oh, you're a load of laughs. I'm sure I can afford it because you will give me a big discount."

"I do have a project I need to finish, but after that, I'd be happy to make something for you as a belated housewarming gift."

"That's very nice of you, Peter."

Sammy had followed them into the living room, waiting patiently at first. When his patience ran out, he let out a demanding meow at Peter. "I'd better feed Sammy before he has a nervous breakdown," Peter said. "Have a seat. I'll be right back."

Hannah sat on the sofa while Peter went into the kitchen, opened a can of cat food, and put it in Sammy's bowl. When he finished, he said from the kitchen, "Would you like a drink?"

"Oh, no. Not while on duty."

"I wasn't talking about alcohol. I have water, iced tea, soda, and orange juice."

"Okay, I'll have a glass of iced tea."

Peter put ice in two glasses and filled them with tea. He carried them to the living room and handed one to Hannah, then sat on the sofa next to her. "I should probably confess that I'm not as cold-hearted as I led you to believe the other day. I would not have turned my back and let people die. It's God that I'm angry with for making me this way."

"I get it," Hannah said. "You needed to show us that you were holding all the cards."

"Yes, because I wanted to spend time with you away from those other guys. Holding all the cards, as you say, was the best way to do that."

"I don't know how to say this nicely, Peter, but.... What I mean to say is, I feel like you like me because I'm the only apple in the bunch that's not rotten."

Peter sighed and shook his head. "That's not true. I understand why you would feel that way, but you shouldn't. There's something about you that's special. Something familiar. I can't explain it."

"Familiar? I was born after you lost your memory, and I don't think we ever met before the other day."

"I told you I can't explain it."

"Maybe you knew someone like me in your previous life."

"I don't know. Maybe."

"Do you think you had this ability in your previous life, or do you think whatever caused your memory loss also caused your ability?"

"That's a good question. I never considered that."

Hannah looked at her watch. "It's getting late. We should probably get going."

***

When they arrived, they parked behind the FBI van across the street from the gym. They entered the van and sat across from Tim and Ben.

Ben turned, smiled, and said, "Hi, guys," before returning his attention to the monitor showing the locker room.

"Anything yet?" Hannah asked.

"No. Nothing yet," Ben said. "It's almost four. Hopefully, something will happen soon."

"So, if this works, and someone opens the locker, what's the plan?" Peter asked.

"Well," Tim said, "since we can't use the video, we need to get him to confess on camera. Ben and I will stop him when he leaves the building while Hannah records him. Once we're sure it's safe, you can come over and ask him questions."

"Maybe I should have a badge and a gun so I don't need to stay behind like a child."

"That won't happen anytime soon," Tim said. "You're too old to begin training as an agent, but if you want to continue helping us, I think some gun training would be in order."

"I may consider it," Peter said.

After a few minutes, Ben said, "I think we got something here."

Everyone looked at the screen. A muscular man in his mid-thirties with short, dark hair approached the locker. He set his gym bag on the bench and looked around before removing the lock and checking inside the locker. He closed it, put the lock back on, picked up his bag, and walked out of sight of the camera.

"We got him," Tim said. "You all know what to do."

They all exited the van. Tim looked at Peter and said, "Wait here until we need you." He looked at Ben and Hannah and said, "Ben, take the left. Hannah, stay with me."

Ben walked past the glass doors and stopped when he reached the side street as if waiting for a ride. Hannah and Tim walked to the business next to the gym, which happened to be a clothing store. They looked at the large window display. To an outside observer, they appeared to be window shopping.

Five minutes later, the man they were waiting for exited the building and turned left. As he approached Tim and Hannah, Tim took out his wallet and gun while Hannah took out her phone and started recording.

Tim flashed his identification to the man. "FBI," he said. "We want to ask you some questions."

The man turned around and saw Ben approaching from the other direction. His left hand held his badge high in the air while his right hand rested over his gun."

The man turned and faced Tim. "What is this about?"

"Please, put your bag down and step away from it."

The man hesitated. His eyes darted between Tim's gun and the bag.

"Put the bag down!" Tim commanded.

The man put his gym bag on the ground.

"Now, step away from it!"

The man took two steps to the left. "It's just my clothes. I was here working out."

"We just want to ask you some questions," Tim said. "You have no obligation to answer. Do you understand?"

The man's eyes narrowed. "Seriously?"

"Tell us you understand you are not required to answer our questions."

"Okay, sure. I understand."

Tim motioned for Peter to come over. He walked to where they were standing and said to the man, "Hello. What is your name?"

"Lee," the man said.

"What is your full name?"

"Leroy Aaron Lucas."

"What's in the bag, Leroy?"

"My clothes," he said. After hesitating, he added, "And money. And also a gun."

"What is the money for?"

"It's payment for drugs."

"What kind of drugs?"

Leroy looked around and back at Peter. "It's for fentanyl."

"So, you are a drug dealer?" Peter asked.

"No. I'm just the courier. I pick up the money one day and bring in the drugs the next day."

"Who do you work for?"

"I don't know his name. I only know he's called 'The Pharmacist.'"

"Where do you bring the money and pick up the drugs?"

"I go to a storage place on Capital called 'Second Room Storage.'"

"What do you do when you get there?"

"I open unit number 412 and put the money inside. The next day, I remove the drugs and distribute them."

"Have you seen this pharmacist? What does he look like?"

"I only saw him once. He's about my age. Average height and skinny. Maybe a little wimpy looking. He has straight, blond hair that's receding at the temples and glasses."

"One more thing," Peter said. What is the lock combination?"

"The combination is two-three-nine-one. It's one of those locks with numbers on the bottom."

"Thank you for your help, Mr. Lucas," Tim said. "I'm sure the judge will consider your cooperation when sentencing you."

"Are you arresting me?" Lucas asked. "I mean, I helped you out."

"We're not arresting you, Mr. Lucas," Tim said. "We don't have time for you. That's why I'm calling the police." He picked up his phone and dialed.

Lucas glared at Tim. "Ungrateful prick."

They waited for the police to pick up Lucas, and then Tim said to Hannah, "You two should check out the storage unit. Ben and I will see what we can learn about this pharmacist guy."

Chapter 7

The storage place was an old mom-and-pop operation, but it was well-maintained with a few modern features. It had a drive-up entry gate keypad that opened a sliding gate. The only other way in was through a door that led to the office. Hannah parked near the office door, and they went inside. The office was clean and smelled of lavender. A counter stretched across the room, except for a small opening on one side. A young woman stood behind the counter, smiling when Hannah and Peter approached. "Can I help you?" she asked.

Hannah held up her identification and said, "We need to know who owns unit number 412."

"I'm sorry. I'm not allowed to give out personal information," the woman said.

"You would be giving it to the FBI," Hannah said, "not some random schmuck that walks in here off the street."

"A rule is a rule," the woman said.

"If we need to get a search warrant, we will get it," Peter said, "but then it will be all over the news that your business is allowing a criminal organization to run an illegal drug distribution center through your facility. I don't think you want that. I'm sure your boss wouldn't want that."

The woman clearly didn't know what to do. Her eyes darted between Hannah and the security camera. She thought for a moment and said, "Well, I guess it wouldn't hurt to show you the name. Please don't tell my boss I did this."

"Our lips are sealed," Hannah said.

When the woman went into the back office, Hannah turned to Peter and said, "I'm impressed."

"I watch a lot of detective shows," Peter said.

The woman returned with a folder and set it on the counter. She positioned herself between the camera and the folder before opening it. "His name is John Smith," she said.

"That sounds fake," Peter said.

"We always get IDs," the woman said defensively.

"Can we see his?" Hannah asked.

"Sure," she said and flipped through the papers until she found it. She handed it to Hannah.

Hannah examined it before showing it to Peter. It was a black-and-white copy of a driver's license. The detail was poor, but it clearly said "John Smith." It also had his photo, but there wasn't enough detail for anyone to positively identify the man. Hannah photographed the license and handed the paper back to the woman. She then texted the photo to Tim and Ben.

"We'd like to see the storage unit," Hannah said.

"That might be pushing it," the woman said.

"What if we said we want to tour the facility?" Hannah asked.

"I guess that would work, but I can't show the storage unit. You'll have to find it yourself." She pushed a button under the counter. The door buzzed, and she said, "Go ahead through."

They walked past several rows of storage units before finding the one they were looking for. It was a small, five-by-five unit. Hannah removed a small evidence bag from her pocket and placed it over the lock.

"What are you doing?" Peter asked.

"If there are fingerprints, I want to disturb them as little as possible."

She flipped the lock up and turned the numbers through the plastic. She opened the lock, removed it, and let it fall into the plastic bag. She then pulled the door up, revealing an empty space.

Peter looked at Hannah. "Do you think they knew we were coming?"

"I don't know. Maybe. It's also possible it has always been empty except for the drugs and money, which would only be here between Monday night and Tuesday morning."

Hannah took out her phone and dialed Tim. "The storage unit is empty," she said when Tim answered. "We need someone out here to dust this place."

"Okay, I'll arrange it," Tim said. "Ben already checked on that license you sent. It's fake."

"That's what we figured," Hannah said. "Did you find any information about the pharmacist?"

"We're still working on it. We found references to a guy called 'The Pharmacist,' but nothing concrete yet."

"Look for a man born on the third of February, 1991," Peter said.

"Okay, we'll try that," Tim said.

When Hannah hung up, she looked at Peter and asked, "Where did you get that date?"

"It's the lock combination."

Hannah looked down at the lock she had set on the floor inside the unit. She looked back at Peter and said, "That's genius."

"I remembered Lucas said they were both around the same age, which means he was born around 1991. It just clicked."

***

The woman, known as "Sunny," sat at her desk, reviewing a budget. She got the nickname from her mother because she was always bright and cheerful. The nickname stuck, but she seemed to have far fewer bright and cheerful days as she aged. She hoped that would change soon.

She reached into her top drawer and took out a Snickers bar. She started to unwrap it when her cell phone rang. It was a number she recognized. "Hello," she said.

The man on the other end of the phone sat behind a massive, dark walnut desk. Its surface, smooth as glass, reflected light from the large window high above the city. He turned and looked out the window as he spoke. "I promised I would help you get what you want, and I keep my promises. I have information that will ensure it. I only need to know that you will keep your promise to me."

"You have my word," Sunny said.

"Okay. I've already sent the information to where it needs to go. You need to act on it."

After he gave Sunny all the details, he hung up and dialed another number. When it was answered, he said, "The FBI is getting too close. We need to move up our plans."

***

Hannah and Peter returned to the FBI field office and met Tim and Ben in the conference room.

"Did you learn anything new?" Hannah asked.

"We sure did," Ben said. "Thanks to Peter's advice, we found our guy. His name's Jeremy Monroe—and get this—he's the mayor's nephew."

Hannah's eyes widened in shock. "You're kidding?"

Ben grinned, shook his head, and said, "Nope. He owns a compounding pharmacy northwest of downtown."

"We requested a search warrant," Tim added. "We should hear something soon."

"A compounding pharmacy seems like the perfect place to produce fentanyl," Hannah said. "He could have drugs where anyone could see them, and nobody would suspect they're not legal."

"I don't understand," Peter said. "If he's producing the drugs at his pharmacy, what do the Mexican drug cartels have to do with any of this?"

"We don't know," Tim said. "That's something we need to find out."

"How would a small-time local pharmacist in Milwaukee get hooked up with a big-time Mexican drug cartel, anyway?" Hannah asked.

"That's another good question," Tim said. "It seems the more we learn, the less we know."

Tim's cell phone rang. He answered it and said, "Tell me some good news." He listened intently and frowned. "What? You've got to be kidding."

Hannah and Peter looked at each other as Tim ran a hand through his hair. "How did they know?"

After a long pause, his expression darkened. "Okay, thanks."

When he hung up, Hannah said, "What is it? What happened?"

Tim looked up, his face still showing signs of shock. He shook his head. "I don't know what happened. The DEA already got a warrant to search the pharmacy. They're there right now."

"What?" Hannah said, shocked. "How in the world did they know before us?"

"I don't know, but we need to get out there and find out," Tim said.

They took separate vehicles to Monroe's pharmacy. It was a small, two-story brick building on a corner lot. The pharmacy occupied the left half, near the corner, while a hair salon occupied the right half.

Several government vehicles were parked in front, including two black vans similar to their FBI van. Further away, a news crew interviewed Alderwoman Sofia Russo. A few agents stood on the sidewalks near the building, keeping the growing crowd of onlookers at bay. A couple of hairdressers and their patrons stood outside the salon watching the commotion.

They had to park a half block away. Tim held up his FBI identification as they walked down the sidewalk toward the pharmacy. He used it to part the crowd of people as they made their way to one of the agents standing on the sidewalk. Tim asked him who was in charge.

The man pointed to a woman standing in the pharmacy doorway, looking at a tablet computer. "Special Agent Jones is our SAC."

They made their way to where Special Agent Jones was standing. Tim showed her his ID and said, "Are you in charge here?"

"Yes. I'm Special Agent Pamela Jones. Why is the FBI involved in this?"

Tim introduced himself and everyone on the team and said, "We believe this pharmacist was dealing with a major drug cartel. We requested a search warrant but learned that you had already obtained one. I'm curious. How did you learn Monroe was producing fentanyl?"

"A courier delivered a package to our office. It contained photos, receipts, ledgers, everything. It must have been from an employee who learned what he was doing."

"You don't know who sent it?" Hannah asked.

"No. It was anonymous," Jones said.

"Do you think we can get a copy of what you have?" Tim asked.

Jones thought for a moment and said, "Well, I guess it wouldn't hurt." She found the files on her tablet, encrypted them, and asked, "Where should I send them?"

Tim handed her a business card, and she sent the files to his email address. "I made the password your last name," she said.

"Thank you," Tim said. "Now, what about Monroe? Do you have him in custody?"

"I'm afraid he wasn't here. We sent agents to his home. His car was there, but it seems he's in the wind."

"Okay," Tim said. "If you find him, please let us know. We have some questions for him."

"You do the same," Jones said.

"What do we do now?" Peter asked as they walked away.

"It's late," Tim said. "Go home. We'll meet in the morning and review the files Agent Jones sent us.

***

Hannah drove Peter home. When she pulled into the driveway, he said, "Would you like to come in? I need to go shopping, but I'm sure I have a couple of boxes of macaroni and cheese or leftover pizza."

Hannah smiled. "While that offer is very tempting, I'm tired and need to get some rest."

"Suit yourself," Peter said. "It's your loss."

"Maybe another time."

Peter was greeted with a series of loud meows when he walked through the door. "Okay, Sammy. I know I'm late. I'm sorry, but I haven't forgotten about you."

Peter grabbed the remote and turned on the television before going into the kitchen. He couldn't see it, but he heard the voice of a newswoman. "Billionaire developer Edward Lancaster says he has not given up on his plans to build a South Shore waterfront shopping district that Mayor Monroe opposes. According to the Mayor, Lancaster's other developments consist of too many bars and nightclubs, which cause problems for the nearby neighborhoods."

Peter took a dish out of the strainer, set it on the counter, and got out a can of cat food. Sammy jumped onto the counter to help speed up the process. Peter opened the can and scooped the food into the bowl, which Sammy eagerly started eating.

"Not on the counter," Peter said as he removed the bowl and placed it on the floor. Sammy jumped down and continued eating.

He opened the refrigerator, found a couple of slices of leftover pizza, and put them on a plate. He didn't feel like cooking anything for just himself. He warmed the pizza in the microwave and carried the plate to the living room. He sat on the sofa just as the news story changed to something that caught his attention. A reporter was interviewing Sofia Russo in front of Monroe's pharmacy. He saw her there earlier but couldn't hear what she said then.

A well-dressed man in his early thirties stood beside Alderwoman Sofia Russo. He said, "We're here in front of Monroe Compounding Pharmacy, which happens to belong to the mayor's nephew, Jeremy Monroe. Twenty minutes ago, the DEA raided this pharmacy because they had evidence that Monroe was producing illegal fentanyl right here at this location. I am here with Alderwoman Sofia Russo, who is campaigning to recall Mayor Monroe. Alderwoman Russo, what do you have to say about today's events?"

He held the microphone in front of Russo, who said, "I have been saying for a long time that the mayor needs to do more about this drug crisis that has plagued the city. Unfortunately for the citizens of this great city, he has done nothing but sit on his hands, and now we know why. His own nephew is the cause of all these problems. Now, I'm not saying that Monroe is directly involved. I don't know if he is or isn't, but what is worse for Milwaukee, a criminal or a fool? Did Mayor Monroe really not know his nephew was involved? If not, was he asleep at the switch?"

"Mrs. Russo. You have been collecting signatures to initiate a recall election. How close are you to collecting the necessary number of signatures?"

"We are very close. I think if the mayor doesn't resign now, which he should, we will be at that number in two or three days, maybe sooner if enough people see this report."

"If you get the necessary signatures, will you run to replace the mayor?"

"That is my intention. I can't sit by and watch this city sink into the abyss when I know I can do something about it."

"Thank you for speaking with us today, Mrs. Russo."

"I'm always happy to talk to the press."

The reporter turned to the camera and said, "There you have it. This is Kevin Reed reporting for Channel 23 News."

Peter changed the channel. He was tired of the news. It was always bad. He wanted to watch something more lighthearted. He flipped through several channels before settling on an old episode of The Big Bang Theory.

Chapter 8

Hannah picked up Peter the following morning. She didn't bother driving to the FBI office to switch cars. Instead, she drove directly to City Hall. They went straight to the mayor's office after a brief delay at a security checkpoint. Hannah showed her ID to the receptionist and said, "We need to speak with Mayor Monroe."

"I'm afraid he's busy at the moment," she said

"It's not a request," Hannah said firmly.

The receptionist straightened in her seat. She paused briefly, appearing conflicted. Then, she nodded, stood, and knocked on the door to the inner office before stepping inside. She returned moments later and ushered them into the office.

Mayor Henry Monroe stood from his desk and greeted Hannah and Peter. He was tall, close to fifty, with thick, graying hair. He was somewhat portly, but he had a handsome face and nearly perfect teeth. "What can I do for the FBI?" He asked. "Is this about my nephew?"

"Yes, it is," Hannah said. "My colleague would like to ask you a few questions."

She turned to Peter, who asked, "Mr. Mayor, did you know anything about what your nephew..." He looked at Hannah.

"Jeremy," she said.

"Yes, Jeremy. Did you know anything about what your nephew, Jeremy, was doing regarding making illegal drugs?"

"I know it looks bad, but I promise you I had no idea about that."

"I believe you," Peter said. "Do you know where he might be right now?"

"I'm sorry. I have no idea. Since his father died a couple of years ago, we haven't stayed in touch too much."

"Do you know of any friends or relatives he might have contacted?" Peter asked.

"I'm afraid not. Both of his parents are dead, and he has no brothers or sisters. As far as friends, I don't know who his friends are. He does have a daughter and an ex-wife. Perhaps you should start there."

"Thank you, Mr. Mayor," Hannah said. She handed him a business card. "Please call me if you hear from him."

"I will," he said. "I know he's my nephew, and I shouldn't feel this way, but I hope you find the son of a bitch."

When they returned to the car, Peter said, "Well, at least we know the mayor wasn't involved in all of this."

"Yeah, but that doesn't help us much."

"Maybe not, but now we don't have to waste time investigating him."

***

They reconvened in the FBI conference room. They sat at the table across from Ben and Tim. Ben stood up, picked up his coffee cup, and looked at Hannah. "I'm gonna get another coffee. Does anyone else want one?"

Hannah held up her mug. "I still have some."

Peter shook his head. "I'm fine."

When Ben returned, Hannah said, "We spoke with the Mayor. He said he knew nothing of his nephew's illegal activities. He also doesn't know where he might be."

"We learned a few things from the files the DEA sent us," Tim said before getting up and dimming the lights. He stood beside the television screen and used a remote to bring up a photograph of two men. It looked like someone took it inside Monroe's pharmacy. Tim pointed to the man on the left. "This is Jeremy Monroe." He then pointed to the man on the right, who was turned so that only part of his face was visible. "We believe this man is Diego Ortiz."

"So Ortiz was in Milwaukee to meet with Monroe," Hannah said.

"Yes," Ben said. "We believe they weren't smuggling drugs into this country, only the raw ingredients. Certain compounds are difficult to get legally in this country, so that's where the drug cartel comes in."

"There's something I don't understand," Hannah said. "Besides the difficulty in someone like Monroe contacting a Mexican drug cartel, why would they bother dealing with someone of no importance?"

"That's something we haven't figured out yet," Tim said.

"Did you learn anything else?" Hannah asked.

"Oh, yes," Tim said before advancing to the next screen. It showed a ledger of supplies, including order dates and quantities. "Over the last several months, Monroe ordered significantly more of certain compounds than in previous months. While his revenue did increase somewhat, it did not increase enough to justify the increase in these compounds.

We checked, and every one of them is associated with fentanyl production."

"So, this only proves something we already knew," Peter said. "The question now is, since Monroe won't be producing any more drugs, are we done here, or are there more pharmacists out there?"

"We are definitely not done," Tim said. "We don't know if there are more pharmacists like Monroe out there, but our focus now is finding him and getting the cartels out of the country."

"What about his phone?" Peter asked. "Can you find out who he called recently?"

"We already requested that information," Ben said, "but it takes time. I doubt we will see anything today."

"What about his family?" Hannah asked. "The mayor said he has an ex-wife and a child?"

"That's right," Ben said. "They split up about two years ago, and his wife moved to Racine with their daughter, who is fifteen now."

"Do you think he might have gone there?" Hanna asked.

"We're in communication with the DEA," Tim said. "They sent agents down there but found nothing useful. They don't think Monroe tried to contact his family."

"Maybe we can check out his house," Hannah suggested. "We might find a clue to his whereabouts there."

"I'm sure the DEA went through everything with a fine-tooth comb," Tim said, "but since there's not much else we can do right now, knock yourself out."

***

Monroe lived in an older but well-maintained neighborhood west of the city, not far from the zoo. The house was a relatively small but attractive two-story brick structure on a wide road with a tree-lined median. They pulled into the driveway and parked behind a newer-model blue Ford Bronco.

The front door had yellow tape across it. Hannah removed the tape and opened the unlocked door. Inside the home, it looked like a tornado had blown through it. Most of the cabinets and drawers were open, and stuff was spewed everywhere.

"It looks like the DEA left no stone unturned," Peter said. "I would guess they took anything relevant."

"You never know," Hannah said. "Sometimes things that seem unimportant to one person might be an obvious clue to another."

They both started looking through the debris. Hannah noticed a picture frame lying upside down on an end table. She picked it up and saw a photo of Monroe with a woman and a girl, perhaps eleven or twelve years old. She showed it to Peter. "This must be his wife and daughter."

"From happier times," Peter said. "I wonder what happened to them."

"I don't know," Hannah said. "It seems most relationships are destined to fail."

Peter looked at Hannah thoughtfully. "I'm sorry about what your father did to you and your mom, but that negative attitude could lead to a self-fulfilling prophecy. That might explain why you have no man in your life."

Hannah placed the picture upright on the table and looked at Peter, annoyed by the comment. "My attitude is not why I'm single. I'll have you know I've had plenty of boyfriends in my lifetime."

"That only confirms it. I bet you end it before they can beat you to it."

Hannah shook her head. "You don't know what you're talking about. You are probably the last person who should be giving relationship advice."

Peter looked out the window and slowly nodded. "You're right. I am not in a position to criticize. I only want you to be happy."

Hannay put her hand on Peter's arm. "I'm sorry, Peter. I shouldn't have said what I said. I know it's not your fault that you have relationship problems, and I appreciate that you care for me. The truth is, you are partly right about me. I do go into relationships expecting them to end, but I don't do anything to cause them to end."

Peter smiled. "Okay. I'm glad we settled that."

Hannah's eyes narrowed. "What is that supposed to mean? Are you patronizing me?"

"No. Of course not. I just think this is a good time to change the subject. I'm sure you don't want to talk about relationships."

Hannah stared at Peter momentarily, then said, "Every now and then, you remind me of my mom. She tries to talk to me like a friend or a sister, but then she'll say something wise, like only a parent would say."

"Being a parent is something I know nothing about."

"Did you ever want to have children?"

After a long pause, Peter nodded. "I did at one time, but it wasn't in the cards."

"It's not too late. You're still young enough. How old are you anyway?"

"I don't know, exactly. A doctor estimated me to be twenty years old, so when they provided me with an identity, they arbitrarily made my birthday the day the priest found me. I officially turned forty-five last month, on the eighth of July."

"Forty-five is not old. You can still have kids."

"I appreciate the encouragement, but I know it's not realistic. Right now, the best thing I can do is to accept that I am what I am, and nothing will change that."

"Well, at least you have someone you can talk to now."

Peter smiled and nodded, "For that, I am eternally grateful."

"Let's do what we came here to do," Hannah said.

They continued to search through the house. While looking through a nightstand in the bedroom, Hannah held up a key fob. "Look at this. It must be a spare key to the Bronco."

"I'm sure they thoroughly searched that," Peter said.

"They thoroughly searched the house, too. What's your point?"

"Okay, let's go look. We're having no luck here."

They went outside, and Hannah hit the button to unlock the vehicle. They heard a muffled thump, indicating she had the right key. Hannah opened the driver's side door while Peter opened the passenger's side. Hannah looked under the seat while Peter checked the glove box. They then checked the back seat and the vehicle's cargo area. When they finished, Peter sat in the passenger seat. Hannah sat in the driver's seat and watched him staring at the dashboard.

"What are you thinking about?" She asked.

"Do me a favor. Start the engine."

Hannah put her foot on the brake and pushed the start button. It roared to life as all the instrument panels turned on, including the radio and navigation system. The Eurythmics blasted through the speakers. "Would I lie to you? Would I lie to you, Honey?"

Hannah and Peter looked at each other and laughed before Hannah hit the button to turn the music off.

Peter entered the settings menu on the GPS system and scrolled through the options.

"What are you looking for?" Hannah asked.

"I'm wondering if his GPS saves where he's been."

"That's a great idea," Hannah said.

After a minute of searching, Peter said, "There is no location history, but there are recent destinations."

Hannah looked at the screen, which showed a list of five addresses. "So these are places he's searched for recently?"

"Technically, they are places he's navigated to, but it doesn't indicate when, so some of these could have been long ago."

"Is the top one the most recent?"

"I think so."

Hannah took a photo of the screen and sent it to Ben before calling him. When he answered, she said, "Ben, I sent you a list of addresses taken from Monroe's vehicle navigation system. They are places that he used the navigation system to find. Check them out. Consider the top address the most recent, and work your way down."

When they returned to the car, Peter asked, "What do you want to do now?"

"I think we should visit Monroe's ex-wife. If she's hiding him, I want to know."

Hannah texted Ben to ask for her address. A minute later, he texted her the address, and she entered it into her car's GPS.

Chapter 9

They arrived at the home in Racine forty-five minutes later. It was an older, two-story house with white siding and burgundy trim. The house seemed small from the front, but it extended far back. A narrow driveway to the left led to a detached two-car garage behind the home. Hannah and Peter ascended the steps to the front porch. Hannah rang the bell, and they waited.

The door opened, and a woman in her mid-thirties appeared. "Can I help you?" she asked.

Hannah showed her ID and said, "Hello. I'm Special Agent Hannah Meyers, and this is Peter Beckett. We're with the FBI. Are you Kathy Monroe?"

"Yes. I assume you are here about Jerry."

"Yes, we are. Can we ask you a few questions?"

She looked at Peter and said, "You don't dress like an FBI agent."

"I've been told," Peter said.

"Peter is a consultant," Hannah said.

"I've already told the other agents everything I know."

"I know," Hanna said, "but we don't know what you told them?"

"Did Jerry contact you recently?" Peter asked.

"I haven't heard from him since he dropped Sophia off on Sunday. Our daughter visits him every other weekend."

"Did you know he was producing illegal drugs?" Peter asked.

"No! Absolutely not! I couldn't believe it when I heard about it. Jerry was an asshole, but he wasn't a criminal."

"Why did you split up?" Peter asked.

Kathy looked inside the house, stepped outside, and closed the door. "When he opened his pharmacy, it occupied all his time. Our relationship suffered. Jerry spent more and more time at the pharmacy. Eventually, I learned he was sleeping with his assistant."

"I'm sorry to hear that," Peter said. "It seems to me that cheating shows bad character. Maybe he was a criminal but hid it well."

"I agree. It does show bad character, but Jerry was intelligent and would not risk doing anything that would send him to jail."

"He must have built up the courage," Peter said.

"I suppose so," Kathy said.

"Do you know where Jerry might be now?"

"I'm sorry. I have no idea."

"Thank you for your time," Hannah said. "That's all the questions we have for you."

"Really?" Kathy asked. "You don't want to check the house?"

"No. We believe you," Hannah said.

"Well, that was another waste of time," Hannah said as they walked back to the car.

"It was a little eye-opening," Peter said before opening his door. They both got in and put on their seatbelts before Peter added, "I mean, how does a guy who is afraid to break the law suddenly become a big-time criminal?"

Hannah shook her head as she started the car. "I don't know. Maybe he needed the money or met someone who influenced him."

"Do you think he has a partner?"

"I was just throwing out ideas, but it's possible."

***

It was well after lunchtime when they headed back, so they stopped for a quick bite to eat at a fast food restaurant on the way. When they arrived at the FBI office, Tim waved them over. "They found Monroe," he said.

"That's great," Hannah said.

"It's not as great as you think. He's dead."

"What? How?" Hannah asked.

"We don't know. We just learned it. We were able to make his autopsy a priority, so we should know more soon."

"Where was he found?" Hannah asked.

"He was behind a laundromat on Center Street. People thought he was a drunk sleeping it off until someone tried to wake him."

"Were there signs of trauma?" Hanna asked.

"We don't know. The details are coming in slowly, but there was no mention of blood or injuries."

"It looks like someone is tying up loose ends," Peter said.

"Yeah. Maybe Monroe had a partner or even a boss," Hannah said.

"I don't know," Ben said. "It's also possible he killed himself to avoid prison."

"Everything is a guess right now," Tim said. "We'll know more when we get the autopsy."

"On another note," Ben said. "I have some information about the addresses you sent me. The oldest one was the Ford dealer, where he bought the car. A salesperson probably put it in to show him how to use it. Considering how long he had owned the car, he didn't use his navigation system very often. The next was to his ex-wife's house. I assume she bought the house after Monroe bought the Bronco. The next two were restaurants, probably not important. The newest one was interesting. It's the U.S. Bank Center."

"Isn't that the tallest building in Milwaukee?" Peter asked.

"Yes. It's the tallest building in Wisconsin," Ben said.

"Why do you think he went there?" Hannah asked. "Did he have an account there?"

"According to his records, he had no ties to U. S. Bank, but there are other businesses in that building," Ben said. "Unfortunately, I couldn't find ties to any of them."

"What other businesses are there?" Peter asked.

"Other financial institutions, law firms, and insurance companies are in the building. There's also a large real estate developer. I couldn't find a relationship between Monroe and any of those businesses."

"Nothing that we know of," Hannah said. "I would keep looking."

"I will," Ben said, "but I'm not sure what else to look for."

"Maybe you should forget Monroe and look at the bigger picture," Peter said.

"What do you mean?" Tim asked.

"What if Monroe was a patsy or fall guy for some bigger purpose? Maybe he was always supposed to get caught. Someone handed Monroe to the DEA on a silver platter. Maybe it was a concerned citizen, or maybe it was part of a bigger plan."

"That gives us something to think about," Tim said.

Hannah touched Peter's arm and said, "You're taking to this job well. You would have made a great agent, even without your ability."

"Who knows? Maybe I was a private eye before my memory loss."

"Yeah, right," Hannah said. "I'm sure you were chasing down leads at twenty years old."

"I wish I could remember."

"Maybe someday you will get those memories back."

"After twenty-five years? Not likely. It's okay, though. I'm focused on the future now, not the past."

Hannah nodded. "That's a good attitude."

"It's because of you. I now have someone I can freely talk to, and I'm helping to solve a crime, although if I weren't here, you would still be in the same position."

"What do you mean by that?" Hannah asked.

"Well, all that work we went through to find Monroe was for nothing since the DEA found him first without my help."

"The DEA was handed Monroe on a silver platter," Tim said. "Nobody could have predicted that. Besides, if your theory is correct, maybe your investigation prompted the person, or persons, to give up Monroe sooner than planned. That means we have them on the ropes."

Hannah rested her chin on her hand. After a long pause, she said, "You guys might be right. It was quite a coincidence that the DEA got their information just as we closed in on Monroe."

"I agree. Someone probably pulled the plug earlier than planned?" Peter said.

"Let's assume it's not a coincidence," Hannah said. "Why would someone turn him in just before he was about to get arrested?"

"Well, if he wasn't a fall guy, maybe he had a partner who worried about going down with him," Tim said. "By turning over evidence, he could later say Monroe coerced him, and that would prove to a court that he was trying to do the right thing."

"So far, the evidence doesn't support that he had a partner other than the drug cartel," Ben said, "although someone must have helped facilitate a meeting between Monroe and the cartel."

"Maybe that person is at the U.S. Bank Center," Peter suggested.

"I'll see if I can find anyone there that might have ties to Mexico," Ben said before turning his attention to his laptop.

Hannah looked at her watch. "There's not much we can do right now. I'm going to take Peter home."

Tim nodded, "Yeah, go ahead. We'll let you know if something comes up."

Chapter 10

As Hannah and Peter drove to work the following morning, Peter said, "I was thinking. I saw the news interview from the pharmacy and wondered how the news crew knew to be there so early. They would have had to know the raid would occur before it happened."

"Let's go ask them," Hannah said.

They stopped briefly to check in with Tim and Ben before driving to the Channel 23 News headquarters. It was a large, two-story building with several satellite dishes on the roof. Hannah didn't park near the front. Instead, she found a side entrance and parked near it. They got out and walked to the door.

"This is the employee entrance," Peter said.

"We're looking for an employee, are we not?"

"Well, since you put it that way."

Peter pulled the heavy metal door open and held it for Hannah. A short hallway opened to a large room filled with cubicles. The low roar of many voices echoed through the air. It reminded Hannah of her high school hallways between classes. The first person they encountered was a young woman who walked toward them carrying a file folder. Hannah stopped her, showed her FBI Identification, and asked where they could find Kevin Reed."

"You want Kevin? Really? Did he do something wrong?"

"No. We need to ask him a few questions," Hannah said. "Do you know where we can find him?"

"Sure," the woman said. "Follow me."

She led them past several cubicles and stopped near two men. The younger of the two sat at a desk and appeared to be editing a video while the other looked over his shoulder.

The woman pointed to the man standing and said, "There he is."

"Thank you so much," Hannah said before the woman resumed her duties.

The two men turned to look when they heard the woman's voice behind them. Hannah showed her ID and asked, "Can we talk to you alone for a minute, Mr. Reed?"

"Of course," Reed said, following them to an area away from people. "I'm not in some kind of trouble, am I?"

"Should you be?" Peter asked.

"Not unless you're from the IRS."

"Do you cheat on your taxes, Mr. Reed?" Peter asked.

"Cheat is a strong word. It's more like fudge."

"Fudge?"

"You know, when you make questionable deductions."

"Mr. Reed," Peter said. "The IRS has a watch list. We will ensure you are on it, so I suggest you don't 'fudge' anything next year."

"Of course. I'll make sure everything is on the up and up."

"My partner is going to ask you a few questions," Peter said.

Hannah furrowed her brow, tilting her head as she looked at Peter, confused.

Peter motioned for her to go ahead.

Hannah looked at Reed and said, "We're here, Mr. Reed, because your news crew was at Monroe's pharmacy fifteen minutes after the DEA raided the place, maybe even sooner than that. The only way you could have arrived so quickly is if you had prior notice that the raid was going to occur. My question is, how did you get that information?"

Reed looked at Peter and then back at Hannah. "You mean you didn't know?"

"Know what? Who told you, Mr. Reed?" Hannah asked.

"We got a call from Sofia Russo. The Alderwoman."

"Did you ask her where she got her information?"

"No. I assumed the DEA told the city leaders what they were about to do."

"As a news reporter, do you make a lot of assumptions?" Hannah asked.

"Well, no, not usually. I suppose I should have dug deeper in this case."

"The first rule of news reporting should be never to trust a politician," Hannah said. "Thank you for your time, Mr. Reed."

When they returned to the car, Peter said, "I take it you are not a fan of politicians."

"I think you are rubbing off on me," Hannah said.

"Me? I never said I didn't like politicians."

"Do you like politicians, Peter?"

"Well, no, but that's not the point."

"Maybe you don't know me better than I know you after all."

"Maybe not," Peter said.

"And what was that about an IRS watch list?" Is there such a thing?"

"I have no idea," Peter said. "I was just trying to scare him."

"I think you did that."

Hannah started the car and drove out of the parking lot. Once they were on the street, Hannah said, "I'm curious. Why did you want me to ask the questions in there?"

"I had confidence in your ability."

Hannah thought for a moment, shook her head, and said, "No, you didn't. You knew Reed was not the kind of guy who would lie to the FBI."

Peter smiled. "Let's go talk to this alderwoman."

***

On the way to City Hall, Hannah said, "It seems like we're getting close. We might be able to wrap this case up in a day or two."

"Are you in a hurry to get rid of me?"

Hannah looked at Peter and put a hand on his knee. "Of course not, Peter, but I know you have your own life to get back to."

"In case you hadn't noticed, my life is not that great. I'm enjoying my time with you."

"I am, too. If we are successful, maybe you can continue working with the FBI as a consultant."

Suddenly, a body fell from the bridge they were about to drive under. Hannah reacted quickly, swerving to the right to avoid it. Unfortunately, her car hit the concrete wall. The airbags deployed before the vehicle rolled twice under the bridge, ending up back on its wheels. When the car came to a stop, and the initial shock had dissipated, Peter looked at Hannah. Her eyes were closed, and he saw a small gash on her forehead. His heart skipped a beat as he quickly unhooked his seatbelt to check on her. He put a hand on her face, and to his great relief, she opened her eyes.

"Are you okay?" she asked.

Peter smiled. "I was about to ask you the same question. You damn near gave me a heart attack."

Hannah put a hand on her shoulder. "I think I reinjured my shoulder."

Several people gathered around their vehicle. A large man tried to open Hannah's door, but it was stuck. He pulled harder, and it flung open. He bent over to look inside. "Is everyone okay?" he asked.

Hannah looked at Peter and back at the man. "Yes. We're okay. Thank you."

She got out of the car but felt wobbly and grabbed the man's arm. He held on to her and said, "Perhaps you should sit down until the paramedics arrive."

"Good idea," Hannah said and sat back in the car.

Peter had gotten out and stood beside Hannah, near the large man. "You should call Tim and Ben," he said. "I'll check on the jumper."

"The jumper was a mannequin," the big man said. He pointed to his right. "It's over there."

"A mannequin? Who would do something like that?" Peter asked.

"People are crazy," the man said.

The traffic was backed up for several hundred feet. About two dozen people were out of their vehicles. Some stood near Peter and Hannah, while others stood near the mannequin. The rest lingered near their cars, trying to catch a glimpse of what was happening. Peter walked to the mannequin. It was face down on the road. Someone dressed it up to look like a female jogger. It had long blond hair tied in a ponytail. It wore black jogging shorts and a white top. It reminded Peter of Hannah the day they met. He rolled it over and was shocked by what he saw. Written in black marker on the shirt was, "Stop right now, or you will find what happens to you won't be kind."

He took out his phone and took a picture of it. He then forwarded the photo to Hannah, Tim, and Ben. He heard sirens as he walked back to the car. Hannah had finished her call and was looking at the photo Peter had sent her. "What the hell?" she said. "Is somebody targeting us now?"

"It would seem so," Peter said.

"That means we're getting close. They're scared."

"They're not the only ones," Peter said.

"Are you scared of these people?"

"Of course, I'm scared of them. A lion will attack when backed into a corner."

"If you want to quit, Peter, I'll understand."

"I'm not afraid for myself. I'm afraid for you."

"It's not your job to worry about me, Peter. I can take care of myself. This is what I trained for."

"Did you train for someone throwing a mannequin off a bridge? We were lucky. That crash could have been much worse."

Two police cars and an ambulance drove on the shoulder past the stopped cars and pulled up close to Hannah and Peter.

"They were just trying to scare us," Hannah said. "Don't worry. This proves they don't want to murder us."

"Not yet, but the closer we get, the more desperate they will become."

Two paramedics approached the car while the police officers spoke to people in the crowd. One of the paramedics asked, "Is anyone injured?"

"I hurt my shoulder," Hannah said.

"She was also dizzy after the accident," Peter said.

The paramedic shone a light in Hannah's eyes. "What is your name?"

"Hannah Meyers,"

"Okay, Hannah. Do you have a headache, nausea, or blurred vision?"

"No, I'm fine."

"Can you stand?"

"Of course," Hannah said and got out of the car. She wobbled and almost fell, but the paramedic held on to her.

He motioned for his partner to help. "We're going to bring you to the hospital. You might have a concussion."

His partner walked along the other side of Hannah and opened the ambulance's back door. After they helped Hannah inside, one of the paramedics asked Peter if he was in the car at the time of the crash.

"Yes," Peter said, "but I'm not hurt."

"We still need to check you out." He told Peter to sit on the back of the ambulance and checked him for injuries. "You seem okay, but if you have any problems over the next few days, I urge you to see a doctor."

"I want to ride along to the hospital if I can," Peter said.

"That should be okay," the paramedic said. "You can ride up front with me."

Hannah spent over an hour in the ER. Tim and Ben showed up to check on her. The doctor told her to take it easy for a while. He also suggested that she not be alone for twenty-four hours.

They rode back to the FBI office with Tim and Ben. When they arrived, they went straight to Hannah's car. Peter insisted that he drive, so Hannah got in the passenger seat.

"You can stay with me for the night," Peter said. "There's a bed in the second bedroom, although I don't know why. No one ever uses it."

"Thanks, Peter, but I can stay with my mom. I have a bedroom there. I should call her and tell her we're coming."

She dialed her mother's number and put her finger to her lips. "Don't say anything about what was on the mannequin."

When her mother answered, Hannah said. "Hi, Mom. I was in a little accident today, and the doctor doesn't want me to be alone for a while. Is it okay if I stay with you?"

"Oh, no! Are you okay, Honey?" Her voice came through the car speakers.

"I'm fine, Mom. I hurt my shoulder and bumped my head, but it's nothing serious."

"Oh, my. What happened?"

"Someone threw a mannequin off a bridge, and I swerved to avoid it. I thought it was a person."

"That's awful! What is wrong with people today?"

"I don't know, Mom."

"Well, I'm glad you weren't hurt worse. You're certainly welcome to stay here. I'll cook a nice dinner. How are you getting here? Is your car okay to drive?"

"My car is fine, but the government car has seen better days. Peter, the guy I told you about, is driving me home."

"Oh, tell Peter he is welcome to stay for dinner. I want to meet him."

Peter looked at Hannah, smiled, and nodded.

"He would love to join us," Hannah said.

"Good. I can't wait to meet him."

When Hannah hung up, Peter said, "Can we stop at my house? I need to feed Sammy."

"Of course," Hannah said. "I wouldn't want Sammy to starve."

Peter parked in his driveway and went inside to feed his cat. Hannah waited in the car. She texted her mother, telling her they had to make a stop and would be there shortly.

Peter returned to Hannah's car a few minutes later and said, "Thanks. Sammy is not happy when his dinner is late."

"You are a good pet parent, Peter."

"He's good company. I have to take care of him."

***

Victor Landa entered his boss's office near the top of the tallest building in Milwaukee. The room was larger than his last apartment. He stepped across the thick, plush carpet and came to a stop before the desk. His boss, Edward Lancaster, looked up, smiled, and said, "How did it go, Vic?"

"I think I scared them pretty well. Only time will tell if they stay scared."

Edward Lancaster was a handsome man who looked younger than his true age. His dark hair and well-trimmed beard were free from gray hairs, and his skin was smooth and without wrinkles. He had his suits tailored to fit his perfectly proportioned frame. When he spoke, people listened. He despised small talk and would only engage in it as a means to an end.

Landa was quite different. His rugged face and a missing front tooth made his smile look menacing. His short, brown hair receded slightly at the temples, and a slightly crooked nose hinted at an improperly set break. What he lacked in beauty, he made up for in brawn. His tall, muscular build, combined with his rugged appearance, exuded a sense of intimidation. He was a man who could make his presence known without saying a word.

Lancaster steepled his fingers and leaned back in his chair. "We need to keep an eye on them. They found someone who can get our people to talk. I've already had to speed up the timetable. Killing FBI agents might draw too much attention to us, but they may leave us no choice."

"I'll do whatever it takes," Landa said, showing his menacing smile.

Landa was fiercely loyal to Lancaster. His life had spiraled downhill since leaving the Marines several years earlier. He wanted to reenlist, but his commander wanted soldiers who could kill when necessary, not soldiers who enjoyed killing. Several months earlier, after seeing a man kick his own dog for moving too slowly, he ended up in jail for beating the man almost to death.

After hearing how harshly Landa protected that dog, Lancaster decided Landa was the perfect man to add to his team. He hired the best criminal attorney in Milwaukee, who got Landa off on a technicality. He then hired Landa as his bodyguard and, for lack of a better term, henchman. He even let him live in his guest house.

Chapter 11

Peter pulled into the driveway of Hannah's mother's house, and they got out of the car. As they walked to the front door, they cast long shadows in front of them.

"This is a nice house. Did you grow up here?" Peter asked.

"I did," Hannah said.

"How did your mom afford it as a single woman raising a child?"

"It belonged to her parents. They died in a car accident about a year before I was born."

"Oh, I'm sorry. That must have been hard, having no dad or grandparents."

"We managed."

Hannah didn't bother knocking. She opened the door and went inside, holding the door open for Peter. No one was in sight, so Hannah called out, "Mom! We're here!"

"I'm in the kitchen, Honey," came her mom's voice. "I'll be right out."

Hannah closed the door and led Peter to the living room, where her mom appeared from the kitchen a few seconds later. She looked a lot like Hannah. She wore a pink blouse and a floral-patterned skirt. Her long, blonde hair was pulled up into a bun.

"Hi, Mom. This is Peter. The guy I've been working with. Peter, this is my Mom, Michelle."

Michelle's jaw hung open as a look of shock passed over her. "Oh, my God!" she blurted, her voice almost a scream.

Peter and Hannah looked at each other, a confused expression on their faces. Michelle ran to Peter and threw her arms around him. She squeezed him tight. After several seconds, she backed away and said, "I knew you would come back one day." She put her hands on Peter's face and kissed him. She pulled away and looked at him while she held his face. "You've aged. How is that possible?"

Peter stepped back and said, "I'm sorry. How do you know me?"

Now Michelle looked confused, "You don't remember me?"

"I told you, Mom, Peter lost his memory. Who do you think he is?"

Michelle looked at Hannah and said, "This is Micah, your father."

It was Hannah's turn to be shocked. She looked at Peter and shook her head. "No, Mom. You're mistaken. Micah left us. This is Peter. He's been living not far from here for the last twenty-five years. A man doesn't leave his family and stay in the same town."

"How many years did you say?" Michelle asked.

Hannah thought for a moment, and then it hit her. "Oh, my God!"

Michelle opened a curio cabinet and removed a small photo frame. She showed it to Hannah and Peter. It was an old photo of Michelle and Hannah's father. Hannah had seen it many times before but didn't make the connection until now. The man in the photo was younger and had longer hair, but it was definitely Peter.

"She's right," Hannah said to Peter. "I knew I had seen you somewhere before. This photo has been in our home since before I was born. I must have looked at it a million times, but never really saw it until now."

Peter took a deep breath. "I think I need to sit down."

Michelle directed him to the sofa and sat next to him. Hannah sat in a chair next to Peter.

Peter looked at Michelle and said, "If I am this Micah guy, tell me what happened on the day I disappeared."

"Well, you were a bit worried. You wouldn't admit it, but I could tell."

"What was he worried about?" Hannah asked.

"He had learned that God was angry with him."

"God was angry with me? Why?" Peter asked.

"For loving me, of course."

"Why would God care that I loved you?"

Michelle studied Peter's face. "Oh, Micah. You really can't remember anything, can you?"

"No, I can't. Tell me why God would be angry because I loved you."

"Because angels are not supposed to have relationships with humans."

"Angels?" Hannah said incredulously. "What are you talking about, Mom? Do you think Peter is an actual angel from Heaven?"

"Of course, Honey. Haven't you been listening to me your entire life?"

"Well, yeah, but whenever you said he was an angel, I thought you were talking figuratively. Like he was a really nice guy."

"Micah was a nice guy, but he could also be tough when he needed to be."

"So, Micah is my real name?" Peter asked. "What's my last name?"

"As far as I know, angels don't have last names."

"Can we get back to what happened?" Hannah asked.

"Oh, yes." Michelle looked at Peter. "Your angel friend, Aziel, told you there would be a meeting with other angels to decide your fate that evening. You told me everything would be fine. That's the last time I saw you."

"Wait! Did you say Aziel?" Peter asked.

"Yes, why?"

A blank expression came over Peter's face. After several seconds, Hannah asked, "Are you okay?"

Peter looked at Michelle. "Where was this meeting to take place?"

"You were supposed to meet them in front of St. Bertilla."

Peter looked at Hannah. "I need to borrow your car. I need to go to St. Bertilla."

"What about dinner?" Michelle asked.

Peter held Michelle's hand and said, "I'm sorry. There's something I have to do."

"If it's important to you, Peter, I'll go with you," Hannah said.

"I'm coming too," Michelle said. "Give me a minute. I have to turn off the stove."

***

They got in Hannah's car. Peter drove, and Hannah sat in the passenger seat. Michelle sat in the back. She slid to the middle so she could see both of them.

"When I met you, Micah, you didn't know how to drive."

Peter looked at Michelle in the mirror. "Really? Driving seemed natural to me when I first tried to drive after my, uh, accident."

"That's because I taught you. You almost wrecked my car a couple of times, but you got the hang of it quickly."

"I guess if I were an angel, I would have had wings and not needed a car."

Michelle laughed. "Angels don't have wings."

"Really? According to the Bible, they do," Peter said.

"The Bible was written by people who sometimes had vivid imaginations," Michelle said. "You told me that."

When they arrived at the church, Peter parked in front, and they all got out of the car. A beautiful orange sky made the perfect backdrop behind the church.

They stepped through the heavy wooden doors. The church was mostly empty, save for a few scattered individuals praying in the pews, some kneeling and some sitting. The scent of incense hung in the air. An elderly priest sat in a chair near the confessional, reading his bible.

Peter walked briskly toward the priest; his loud footsteps on the marble floor echoed across the sanctuary. A few of the parishioners looked up to see what the commotion was. Hannah and Michelle raced to keep up with Peter.

When Peter got close, the old priest looked up and said, "Good evening. It seems something important is on your mind. How can I help you?"

"Something important is on my mind. I need to speak with Father Aziel. It's urgent."

Hannah and Michelle caught up to Peter and stood behind him.

"I'm afraid there is no Father Aziel here," the priest said.

"Okay. Where is he?"

"You don't understand. There is no Father Aziel at this church. Are you sure you are in the right place?"

Peter's eyes narrowed. "Of course, I'm in the right place. Father Aziel has been here for twenty-five years. I gave a confession to him right here a few days ago."

The priest slowly shook his head. I'm sorry, son. I have been here almost thirty years and never heard that name before."

Peter turned to look at Hannah and Michelle. Hannah shrugged. Peter turned back to the priest. "I'm sorry. Thank you for your time."

As they left the church and walked to Hannah's car, Peter said, "I don't understand it. Father Aziel found me the night I lost my memory. He helped me get on my feet. I have been coming here to see him ever since. How could that priest not know him?"

"Maybe he's lying to you," Hannah offered.

Peter looked at Hannah, who said, "Oh, yeah. I forgot."

"I told you Aziel is your angel friend," Michelle said.

They reached Hannah's car and climbed in. When they got on the road, Michelle put a hand on Peter's shoulder and said, "I think I know what happened to you. Your punishment was to live as a human without the memory of who you were. That's why you've aged. Your friend, Aziel, has been there to help you through the tough times. Now that the truth has exposed him, he can no longer help you, but I can. I know you don't remember me, Micah, but I promise you can trust me."

Peter looked at Michelle through the mirror. "I appreciate that, Michelle, but I'm not sure I believe any of this."

"I don't know if I believe it either," Hannah said, "but it would explain your ability and why I'm immune to it."

"What ability?" Michelle asked.

"People can't lie to Peter," Hannah said.

"Hmmm, interesting," Michelle said.

"Does that surprise you, Mom?"

"A little. I assumed he would have lost his angel powers when he became human."

"You mean he had that power when you knew him before?"

"Of course. All angels do."

"So, it didn't bother you that you couldn't lie to him?"

"Of course not, Honey. I never had a reason to lie."

"You used the word 'powers,'" Peter said. "Did I have more than one?"

"You did have one other ability that I knew of, but it only worked on certain people."

"What was that?" Peter asked.

"Well, you could command people to do something, and they would obey."

"Really? I've never noticed that ability. Did it come up when we were together?" Peter asked Michelle.

"It did once. You came to my work to meet me for lunch. That was when I worked as a front desk clerk. You saw a guest giving me a hard time because the air conditioner in his room was not working. I told him I would send a maintenance guy to his room, but that wasn't good enough. He wanted another room. I told him we were full, but he didn't believe me. He called me a dumb blonde. That's when you stepped in. You demanded he apologize and then go to his room and shut up. He immediately did both of those things."

"Wow!" Peter said. "I can't imagine myself ordering people around like that."

"You were my hero."

"You don't strike me as someone who needs a hero, Michelle."

Michelle leaned back in her seat. "I'm no longer that nineteen-year-old girl that you knew. After you disappeared, I needed to grow up fast."

Peter shook his head and said, "I'm sorry, Michelle. If I had known..."

"Stop!" Michelle said. "It wasn't your fault."

"You said that power only worked on certain people. What kind of people?" Peter asked.

"You told me the further someone was from God, the more easily you could influence them."

"You mean like bad guys?"

"Something like that," Michelle said.

When they returned to Michelle's house, she finished cooking dinner. They sat at the table, and Michelle said grace before they dug in.

"After everything that happened tonight, I'm not sure how we should move forward," Hannah said to Peter. "I mean, do we go back to the way things were? What do I even call you? Should I call you 'Dad'? Should I call you 'Peter'? What about 'Micah'?"

"Wait! Slow down," Peter said. "This is confusing for me, too. Let's not change anything just yet."

"So, you are okay with continuing the case with me?"

"Of course," Peter said. "I like spending time with you. Now that I know you're my daughter, I want that even more. But you need to take tomorrow off. You had a concussion. You need to heal first."

"That's right," Michelle said. "The FBI can survive a day without you."

"I think I need a day off, too," Peter said. "Maybe we can all hang out tomorrow."

Michelle smiled. "It is so great having you back, Micah, or should I say 'Peter?'"

"Whatever name you are comfortable with is fine with me," Peter said.

"Okay, then. Micah, it is."

"Tell me, Michelle. How did we meet?"

"You saved my life. I was crossing the street not far from St. Bertilla's. I didn't see the truck that had run the red light, but you did. You grabbed me and pulled me back just in time. At the time, I thought I was there alone. It was like you appeared out of nowhere."

"Oh, so I was like a guardian angel?"

"That's what I thought, but you told me there was no such thing as guardian angels. You said angels don't hang around people waiting for something bad to happen."

"So, why was I there?"

"You said that I distracted you with my beauty. You said you followed me because heaven had nothing that compared to me. I'm sure that wasn't true, but you were quite the charmer."

"I don't know what heaven looks like, but if I said it, I'm sure it's true."

Michelle smiled. "You're still a charmer."

After dinner, they sat in the living room and talked for a long while. Peter yawned, looked at his watch, and said, "It's getting late. I should get going."

"You can take my car," Hannah said.

Everyone stood, and Peter hugged Michelle. "Thank you for that delicious dinner," he said. "Today will go down as one of my most memorable, in more ways than one."

"Your return has made me very happy, Micah."

"I'll walk you out, " Hannah said, following Peter out the door. "So, what do you think of Mom?"

"I think she's a lovely lady."

"Do you think she's right? Do you think you are an angel, or at least used to be?"

"I guess it's possible, but it seems far-fetched. What if your mom is some kind of wackadoodle, and this is all part of her delusion?"

Hannah slapped Peter's arm. "Mom is not a wackadoodle. You take that back."

"I'm sorry. I like your mom. I think she's great, but I have a hard time believing I'm an actual angel, or at least used to be."

"It would explain a few things," Hannah said. "It perfectly explains why you can compel people to tell you the truth and why I'm immune to your power. It also explains why your priest friend only exists in your head."

"He doesn't exist only in my head. He's real."

"Real or not, he made you believe he was a priest in that church. That sounds like something an angel could do."

"Are you telling me you believe all of this?"

"I'm telling you my mind is open to the possibility. Yours should be, too."

"Okay. I'll try to keep an open mind."

When they reached Hannah's car, Peter leaned over and kissed her on the cheek. "I had a nice evening. It was quite eye-opening."

"That's the understatement of the year."

Chapter 12

Peter drove Hannah's car to Michelle's house the following morning. He passed a florist on the way and decided to stop. He pulled the door handle, but the door was locked. He looked at the hours printed on the window and then at his watch. He was three minutes early. An older woman, perhaps in her mid-sixties, saw him at the door and unlocked it for him.

"I'm sorry," Peter said. "I didn't realize I was too early."

"It's perfectly fine, young man. Come on in."

Peter stepped inside the floral shop. It was neat and clean, with a large counter straight ahead. A table stood in front of the window, holding a variety of potted plants. Along the left wall were two large refrigerators with glass doors. Inside were several flower bouquets. The right wall held several shelves displaying vases of various sizes and styles. A rack holding about a dozen varieties of flowers stood between Peter and the right wall.

The woman stepped behind the counter and asked, "How can I help you this morning?

"Well, I ran into a woman I haven't seen in twenty-five years yesterday, and today, we are going to spend the day together."

"Is she a friend or a former lover?"

"She is someone I once loved, but circumstances prevented us from being together."

"Oh, and now you have a second chance at love. How romantic."

"Can you suggest something that would be appropriate for the situation?"

She stepped out from behind the counter and pointed at some flowers. "How about some Peruvian lilies? They symbolize friendship and devotion. We can include a few pink roses for admiration. Oh, and tulips would be a great addition. They symbolize a new beginning, which sounds like what you are hoping for."

"I'm not sure what I'm hoping for, but a new beginning might be what I need."

"I can have these ready this afternoon or put it together now for a small rush charge."

"I'm happy to pay the rush charge to get them right away."

Peter paid for the flowers and waited. Ten minutes later, the woman handed the flowers to Peter. They included a lovely vase. "These are beautiful," Peter said. "Thank you so much."

"I think she will love them," the woman said. "Good luck."

Peter placed the flowers on the front seat and gently held them in place with his hand to keep them upright while he drove. When he arrived at Michelle's house, he rang the bell and waited.

Hannah answered the door and said, "Good morning, Peter. Oh, you brought flowers. They're beautiful. Are those for Mom?"

"Yeah. I know it's not much, considering I disappeared when she needed me most."

"She knows that's not your fault. Come on in."

Peter stepped inside, smiled, and kissed Hannah on the cheek. "You look beautiful this morning," he said.

"You're in a surprisingly good mood," she said as she stepped aside to let him in. "I thought last night might have freaked you out a little bit."

Peter studied Hannah's face briefly and asked. "Did it freak you out?"

"Maybe a little. I mean, I lived my entire life believing my father walked out on me, and suddenly, I learned he was an angel, and I've been working with him. What are the odds of that?"

Peter smiled. "Well, I'm not a math whiz, but I would estimate the odds are about a hundred percent, at least the part about working with me."

"You know what I mean. It's a big city. The odds of us meeting like this are a million to one."

"Maybe God put us together."

Hannah looked at Peter, surprised. "Are you starting to believe now that you're an angel?"

"I spent a lot of time thinking last night and realized it doesn't matter what I am. I was in church the day we met because I wanted God to remove the burden he had given me. Now I feel like he's done that."

"But nothing's changed. You still have the same ability. At least, I think you do."

"Yes, but I'm sure you have heard that God's ways are not our ways. I thought the only way God could help me was to remove this so-called gift, but I was wrong. God gave me a beautiful daughter and a wonderful woman who loves me and is not bothered by what I am. What could be better than that?"

"You didn't seem terribly excited to be around Mom last night. You called her a wackadoodle."

Peter looked around. "Is she here?"

"She's upstairs getting ready."

"I said she might be a wackadoodle, and I feel bad about that now. It took me a while to realize how special she must be. I never met a woman who still wanted to be with me after learning about my ability."

"She is special, and you better never forget that."

"I certainly won't."

Hannah took the flowers from Peter and set them down on the coffee table. She took out her phone and said, "I should probably check in with Tim and Ben."

She dialed Tim's number. When he answered, he said, "Good morning, Hannah. How are you feeling today?"

"I feel fine, except for a slight pain in my shoulder. Call me if you need me, but I'm going to take the doctor's advice and take the day off just in case."

"I don't blame you. That was quite an accident you two were in. Will Peter be coming in?"

"No. He's here with me. After what happened last night, we both needed to clear our heads. He needed the day off, too."

"Last night? The accident was in the afternoon. Are you okay?"

"I'm not talking about the accident," Hannah said.

After a long pause, Tim asked, "Are you going to string me along, or will you tell me what happened?"

"Well, Peter took me to my mom's house, and he stayed for dinner." Hannah paused, searching for the right words.

"And...," Tim said.

"And it turned out my mother knew him from before his accident. Before he lost his memory." She paused again.

"Okay...," Tim said slowly. "Who is he?"

"His name is Micah. He's my father."

"What? You're kidding?"

"No. I'm not kidding."

"Wow! Well, if that's true, that would explain why you are immune to him," Tim said. "Whatever he has, some of it has been passed down to you."

"Maybe, but nobody feels compelled to tell me the truth."

"That might be a good thing," Tim said. "It sounds like that ability is quite a burden for Peter, or Micah, or whoever he is."

"I think we should stick with Peter for now," Hannah said.

"Well, if you're up to it, I guess we will see you both tomorrow," Tim said.

"Okay. In the meantime, maybe you can ask Alderwoman Russo how she knew the DEA would raid Monroe's pharmacy before it happened." Hannah said.

"Okay. We'll do that."

As Hannah hung up the phone, Michelle descended the stairs and entered the living room. She saw the flowers and looked at Peter, saying, "Oh, those are beautiful. You are so thoughtful, Micah."

She kissed Peter. It was a long, lingering kiss. After a few seconds, Hannah looked away. "Okay, Mom. You two are not alone here."

Michelle pulled away. "I'm sorry, Honey. I was just showing my appreciation."

"Well, show your appreciation when I'm not around."

"Hey, why don't we all go out for breakfast?" Peter suggested. "My treat."

"I would love that, Micah," Michelle said.

"I'm driving this time," Hannah said.

"The doctor wanted you to be careful for a full day," Peter said.

"I'm fine," Hannah said. "I haven't felt dizzy since I was at the hospital."

"This must be what a snow day feels like," Peter said. "All play and no work."

"I'm not complaining," Hannah said. "This is the first time in my life I have been able to spend a day with my mom and dad together."

"Maybe we should go to the park and get ice cream later," Peter suggested.

"I know you're joking, but that's a good idea."

They drove to a restaurant Peter had been to several times before. It was a stand-alone building next to a bank. He was familiar with the place because he had an account at the bank next door. The lot was mostly full, so Peter parked behind the building, and they walked to the front. They had to wait a few minutes, but when a table was ready, the friendly hostess led them to it and set down their menus. "Your server will be with you shortly," she said.

"I think it's pretty great that you two are working together," Michelle said. "The way you met was quite a coincidence."

"I'm not so sure it was a coincidence," Peter said.

"Really? Do you think God put you two together?"

"I don't know, Michelle, but I think it's possible."

"If that's true, maybe God is no longer angry with you."

"I doubt it. I had some choice words for God the other day."

"Last night, you said you were at that church to confess the day you met Hannah. God forgives. Perhaps he forgave you after your confession."

"Hannah was assigned to recruit me before I went to the church to confess. If he put her there, then God can see the future."

"Some people believe that he can," Michelle said. "Or perhaps God saw that you reached a breaking point and decided he had punished you enough."

"That makes the most sense if any of this is even true."

"Do you think what I told you about being an angel is not true? You know I can't lie to you."

The server interrupted them, saying, "I'm sorry for the wait. We're pretty busy today. Can I get you some coffee this morning?"

They all said they wanted coffee. When the server left, Peter said, "I know you believe I'm an angel, but what if I lied to you? What if I told you that to impress you?"

"You saved my life," Michelle said. "Nothing you could have said would have impressed me more after that."

"It just seems unbelievable to me that I could be an actual angel."

"It is unbelievable to you because you are human now and no longer remember your previous life. It would be like imagining yourself as a fish."

Peter laughed. "You might be right about that. I'm not a good swimmer."

"That reminds me," Hannah said. "You need to go to Peter's house and see some of his animal carvings. They're beautiful."

"Oh, you're an artist now? That's great, Micah. I always knew you were good with your hands," Michelle said.

"I make custom furniture for a living. The carvings are just a hobby."

"I can't wait to see them."

The server returned with their coffee and then took their order. When she left, Michelle said, "I know what you are, Micah, or were, but I understand why you have doubts."

Peter took Michelle's hand and looked her in the eyes. "What I don't doubt is that I am blessed to have someone who loves me. I don't remember ever having that before."

They both leaned toward each other and kissed. It was a soft, tender kiss. Michelle put her hand on Peter's face and said, "I will always be here for you."

"So will I," Hannah added.

Peter took both of their hands and said, "Since I woke up that day twenty-five years ago, this is the happiest I have ever been."

***

Being from Washington, Tim and Ben didn't have their own desks at the Milwaukee office, so they sat in the conference room. Ben opened his laptop and said he had investigated the businesses inside the U.S. Bank Center further but could find no link to Monroe or Mexico. He also said the autopsy results were in on Monroe, and he died of a fentanyl overdose.

"Really?" Tim said. "What are the odds of that being an accident?"

"Pretty low," Ben said, "because he had enough of the drug in his system to kill an elephant. It was probably suicide. He might have felt that death was better than prison."

"I don't think so," Tim said. "I think Peter was right. Someone was tying up loose ends. Why would he kill himself behind a laundromat in an area nowhere near his home or business? And how did he get there without a car? What about the information that fell into the laps of the DEA? Have we learned where that came from yet?"

"So far, that seems to be a dead end," Ben said.

"Since Hannah and Peter will be out today, we need to get out in the field."

They drove to city hall and found Sofia Russo's office on the third floor. When they got off the elevator, there was a security checkpoint. The two agents showed their IDs to the guard, who informed them that they would need to leave their weapons with him. They did so reluctantly. Tim had become used to carrying a gun and felt comfortable knowing it was there.

A young man sat at a desk outside Russo's office. It surprised Tim that a simple Alderwoman would need an assistant, but there he was. They all showed their IDs and told the young man they needed to speak with Sofia Russo. He nervously got up, knocked on her door, and entered her office. When he returned, he said, "You can go in now."

Sofia Russo stood and greeted the two men as they entered her office. "I must say I am surprised by your visit," she said. "What can I do for the FBI?"

"First, thank you for seeing us, Ms. Russo," Tim said.

"Mrs.," Russo said. "I've been married for twenty-five years."

"Of course," Tim said. "Thank you for seeing us, Mrs. Russo. We're here to find out how you knew about the raid on Monroe's pharmacy before anyone else knew about it."

"I didn't realize I did know it before anyone else."

"You called a news team and were there being interviewed by them twenty minutes after the raid took place," Tim said. "You must have known it would take place before it happened."

"Someone called me a few hours earlier, saying the DEA would raid Monroe's pharmacy and that I should be there."

"Who called you?" Tim asked.

"I don't know. He didn't give me his name. After he called, I looked up the pharmacy's owner and learned it was the mayor's nephew. That's when I knew he was trying to help my cause to recall the mayor. He probably works with the DEA or for the judge who issued the warrant."

"Does your phone remember the caller IDs?" Ben asked.

"The calls come to the main phone number and are then routed to my office. You could probably get a list of numbers that called City Hall, but that list would be huge."

"Could you identify his voice?" Ben asked. "Did you hear it before?"

"No. I don't think so. I talk to so many people. There's no way I could remember them all. I can say that he sounded like he had a local accent. Like he grew up here."

"Is that it?" Tim asked. "Can you think of anything else that might be helpful?"

Russo thought momentarily and said, "No. That's all I can remember."

"Thank you for your time, Mrs. Russo. We'll be in touch if we have any more questions."

After they left Russo's office, Tim asked, "What do you think? Do you believe her?"

"I think she knows more than she's telling us," Ben said.

"I agree. I think Hannah and Peter need to question her tomorrow."

Chapter 13

After breakfast, Michelle asked, "Since you two have the day off, what would you like to do?"

"I would like to learn about what you two have been doing without me for the last twenty-five years," Peter said. He looked at Hannah, "Where did you go to school? Who are your friends? What did you do for fun when you were young?"

"That is a lot for one afternoon," Hannah said, but I can take you to where I went to school."

Peter looked at Michelle. "I also want to see where you work. Maybe it will spark a memory."

"Okay," Michelle said. "If you could remember something, that would be great."

Hannah drove past her elementary school, middle school, and high school. They were relatively close together, which allowed her to show Peter everything in less than twenty minutes. They then drove to the hotel where Michelle worked. Since she called in sick, she didn't want to go inside. Peter had seen the hotel before and tried to remember when he had last visited to see Michelle, but the memory wouldn't come.

They returned to Michelle's house. It was approaching lunchtime, so Michelle made sandwiches for everyone. While she was doing that, Peter asked Hannah, "Can I see your bedroom?"

"My bedroom? Why do you want to see that?"

"You can learn much about someone by looking at their bedroom."

"If you want to know something about me, just ask."

"Are you afraid to show me your bedroom?"

"No. I'm not afraid of anything."

"Okay, then. Let's go."

Hannah reluctantly led Peter up the stairs to her bedroom. It looked exactly like Peter would have guessed a teenage girl's bedroom would look like. A double bed sat in the center of the room against the far wall, under a window. It had a white frame with a headboard covered in hearts. The comforter was a teal color. There were two pillows with a third decorative pillow in front. Embroidered on the front pillow were the words, "A Princess Sleeps Here." Peter turned around and saw Hannah leaning against the door with a suspicious look on her face. "What are you hiding there?" he asked.

"What do you mean? What makes you think I'm hiding something?"

Peter grabbed the door and tried to close it, but Hannah leaned harder against it. "You are hiding something."

"Okay, fine," Hannah said, moving aside.

Peter closed the door and saw a Twilight poster hanging on it. "Team Jacob, huh? So, you like the wolf boy?"

"I was sixteen when I hung that there."

"There's no need to be embarrassed. I think it's cute."

"Great. Now I'm even more embarrassed."

Peter laughed. "Is that why you don't have a boyfriend? Are there no single werewolves around here?"

Hannah playfully slapped Peter's arm. "Stop! That's why I didn't want you to see that. I knew you would tease me."

"I'm sorry," Peter said. "I'm sure when I was a teenager, I did things I would be embarrassed about today."

"I always assumed angels started as adults like Adam and Eve."

"Are you saying now you believe I was an angel?"

"No, I'm not saying that, exactly. I don't know what I believe."

"You know, if you're looking for a boyfriend, I think Ben is available. I know he's not a werewolf, but..."

"Ben? Seriously? I'm not going to date someone I work with. Besides, he works in Washington and will be going back when this case is over."

"Well, if you change your mind, I think he's interested in you."

"How would you know that?"

"I've seen the way he looks at you."

"Lunch is ready," Michelle yelled from downstairs.

"I guess we can continue this conversation later," Peter said.

"Hopefully, much later."

***

Tim and Ben stopped for lunch and then returned to the FBI field office, where they conducted further research on the mannequin incident. After some time, Ben said, "Look at this."

Tim stood behind Ben and looked at his laptop screen. "A witness reported that they saw an older model, dark-blue Chevy Malibu parked on the bridge at the time of the incident," Ben said. "There are no cameras near that overpass, but based on the direction in which the car was parked, we know it was traveling east."

"Okay," Tim said slowly. "How does that help us?"

"Well, I looked for cameras along the highway to the west and found one about a mile away. There is an onramp between the camera and the overpass, so I couldn't see every car, but I did see a car that matched the description at around the right time."

Ben brought up a video of the car driving by. He paused the video and enlarged the area around the license plate. It was pixelated, but the number was readable. "You need to find out who owns that vehicle," Tim said.

"I already did that," Ben said, bringing up another screen. It was a scan of a driver's license. The name on the license was Victor Landa.

Tim studied the photograph. "You know, this guy looks a little like Diego Ortiz. Can you bring up the photo of Monroe with Ortiz?"

Ben found the photo and displayed it next to the driver's license. Tim studied both images. "I think it's the same guy. Bring up the other photo of Ortiz with Salvador Salinas."

Ben found the photo and opened it. Tim studied all three images. After a while, he said, "I don't think the man with Monroe is Ortiz. Landa has a more tapered chin, and his hair is receding slightly more than Ortiz's. It's subtle, but it's there. I also think Landa might be taller than Ortiz. Look how much shorter Monroe is than the other guy."

"So, you think that is Landa with Monroe?" Ben asked.

Tim studied the images further. "Yes. I think that's Landa."

"Oh, shit!" Ben said. "If it's true, the cartels were probably not involved. Someone probably wanted everyone to be looking in the wrong direction. That means our entire reason for being here is out the window."

"Do you want to quit now, or do you want to see this through?"

"Of course, I want to finish what we started."

"Okay, then. We do not need to include this new knowledge in our official report. Did you learn anything else about Landa?"

"I learned he served one tour in Iraq and then got an RE-4."

"An RE-4? What's that?"

"It means he was not eligible to reenlist."

"Really? Does it say why?" Tim asked.

"No. There is no mention of why he was not allowed to reenlist. I could submit a request with the Marines, but that would take a while. It's probably unnecessary anyway. I think it's a good guess that his commanding officer thought he was unstable or unpredictable."

"Great," Tim said. "That's all we need, a lunatic Marine after one of our agents. What else does it say about him?"

"It seems he has bounced from job to job since coming home. He is currently listed as unemployed, but if he's working under the table, we wouldn't know about it. It also said he was charged with aggravated battery for severely beating a man, but his lawyer got him off on a technicality."

"That's interesting," Tim said.

"It gets better," Ben said. "I looked up his attorney. He's considered one of the best in the city. How does a guy like Landa afford someone like that?"

"Maybe he works for someone rich and powerful. Does it list his current address?"

Ben looked at his screen. "Yeah. He has an apartment on 38th Street."

Tim stood and said, "Okay. Let's go talk to him."

***

Landa's apartment was in an old, brick three-story building on a corner lot. They drove around to a small parking lot behind the building. When they got out, Ben looked at the building and shook his head. "I don't think Landa works for someone rich and powerful. How can people live like this? The landlord should be arrested."

Some of the windows were boarded up, and a couple more were cracked. One window had a curtain. The rest were covered with sheets or left uncovered. Weeds pushed their way through the dozens of cracks in the pavement while trash littered the entire area.

"If this place were any better, the rent would be higher, and half these people would probably be living on the streets," Tim said.

"That's a shame."

"Yes, it is, but some of these people are probably battling addictions and are lucky to have a roof over their heads. It's even possible the people we are trying to stop caused some of those addictions."

They went inside. The hallway was dimly lit. A few of the fluorescent lights were out while others flickered and hummed. The once white paint was now various shades of yellow. The air was damp with a strong, musty odor that mixed with the smell of cigarette smoke. The apartment they were looking for was the second door on the right. Tim knocked, and they waited.

Thirty seconds later, the door across the hall creaked open. A man in his late fifties stepped into the corridor. He was of average build, with a weathered face, unkempt gray hair, and a scruffy gray beard. The man lingered momentarily before saying, "Are you boys looking for an apartment? You should know we don't see people like you around here too often."

"People like us?" Ben asked.

"Yeah. You know. Well dressed. I assume you're gay, but that's okay. Nobody judges around here."

"Tim showed his ID to the man. We're with the FBI. We're looking for your neighbor, Victor Landa."

"Vic? He's gone. Left a few weeks ago. Just disappeared. No notice or nothing. He left half his stuff behind. Not that he had much to begin with."

"Do you know where he moved to?" Ben asked.

"Nope. Sorry. He didn't talk to people much."

"Thank you for your time," Tim said.

When they returned to the car, Tim said, "We need to get the police to put out a BOLO on Landa's car.

Chapter 14

"Good morning, my dear, Peter said as he got in Hannah's car the next morning. "I had a great time with you and your mom yesterday."

"I did, too, but today, we need to focus on our job. I spoke with Tim this morning, and they learned who was responsible for the mannequin incident the other day."

"Oh yeah? Should we go talk to him?"

"How do you know it was a man?"

"I don't. Was it a woman?"

"No. It was a man."

Peter shook his head. "As I was saying, should we go talk to him?"

"Unfortunately, they don't know where he is, but I'm sure we will find him eventually. They think he was the one in the photo with Monroe, not Ortiz."

"Really? So, is the drug cartel involved at all in this?"

"We don't know yet, but it's looking less likely."

When they arrived at the FBI office, Tim and Ben discussed what they had learned the previous day about Landa. Tim then said, "We spoke with Alderwoman Russo. She was not exactly a treasure trove of information. We thought you would have better luck with her today."

"I'm sure we will learn something from her," Hannah said.

When the discussion was over, Hannah and Peter headed to City Hall. After going through security and dealing with Russo's gatekeeper, they were ushered into her office.

Alderwoman Russo greeted them warmly when they entered. "Please, have a seat," she said, motioning to the two chairs in front of her desk.

Hannah and Peter sat down. Russo's desk was cluttered with papers and file folders. Peter noticed the nameplate on the desk that read "Sofia 'Sunny' Russo." He wondered where the nickname came from.

"I spoke with your colleagues yesterday," Russo said. "Did they not tell you?"

"Yes, they did," Hannah said. "They also thought you were hiding information."

Russo feigned shock. "Really? Why would they think that?"

Hannah looked at Peter as if to say it was his turn.

Peter leaned closer to Russo's desk and said, "Ms. Russo..."

"Mrs.," Russo said.

"Sorry. Mrs. Russo, who told you there would be a raid on Monroe's pharmacy?"

After a short pause, she said, "Edward Lancaster."

"That name sounds familiar," Hannah said. "Who is he?"

"He happens to be the richest person in Milwaukee, maybe in all of Wisconsin," Russo said.

"That's right," Peter said. "He owns that big real estate development company, uh..."

"Lancaster Smith Development," Russo said.

"That's right," Peter said. "Who is Smith?"

"Smith was a former partner who died in a tragic accident years ago. Lancaster kept his name out of respect for him," Russo said.

"Okay, how did Lancaster know the DEA would raid the pharmacy?"

"I have no idea," Russo said. "He's rich. I'm sure he has sources of information that most people can't get."

"So why would he tell you this?" Peter asked.

"Because he has supported this movement to remove Monroe from the beginning."

"I think I understand now," Peter said. "I saw a news story the other day that said Mayor Monroe was against a development project on the South Shore. I assume that was Lancaster's project."

"That's right. It would have been great for the city."

"So, I take it you support the project, which is why he is helping you. If you replace Monroe, Lancaster can get his project built."

"That's right."

"So essentially, Lancaster bought you," Hannah blurted out.

"That is not true!" Russo snapped. "He has not given me a dime."

"He's given you information," Hannah said. "You are just a means to an end. He's using you."

"Oh, get off your high horse," Russo said. "He's done nothing illegal, and neither have I. This is how politics work in America. Love it or leave it."

Peter could see Hannah's anger rising, so he put his hand on her shoulder and said, "I'll take care of this."

"Mrs. Russo," Peter said. "Whose idea was it to attempt a recall on Mayor Monroe? Was it your idea or Lancaster's?"

"Lancaster came to me with the suggestion. I thought it was a great idea, so I went with it."

"Thank you for your time, Mrs. Russo," Peter said.

When Hannah and Peter left, Russo picked up her cell phone and called Lancaster. When he answered, she said, "The FBI was here again. I'm sorry, but I told them what they wanted to know this time. I don't know why. It was like I couldn't resist."

"It's okay. I know all about it."

***

When Hannah and Peter reached the elevator, Hannah said, "What do you think this Lancaster has to do with anything?"

"I don't know," Peter said. "Let's go ask him."

Once back in the car, Hannah got out her phone and searched for Edward Lancaster. Lancaster Smith Development was at the top of the list that came up. She clicked on the link and entered the address into her car's GPS. When the map came up, Hannah looked at it and said, "Holy shit."

Peter looked at her, confused. "What? What's the matter?"

"Lancaster Smith Development is in the U.S. Bank Center."

"What? You're kidding?"

"Nope."

"Well, I think that explains the connection," Peter said.

"Not fully," Hannah said. "It shows Lancaster is somehow associated with both Jeremy Monroe and Sofia Russo, but I don't understand the connection."

Peter smiled but said nothing. Hannah looked at him and asked, "What are you grinning about?"

"I figured out something before you did."

"Oh, don't be a child. What did you figure out?"

"Think about it," Peter said. "If you were Edward Lancaster and wanted to get your project approved, but the mayor was standing in your way, how would you get rid of him?"

Hannah thought momentarily and said, "Well, I would do exactly what he did and convince a politically connected supporter to conduct a recall campaign."

"Yes, but that campaign won't work unless the city is suffering under the current mayor's leadership."

Hannah thought for a long moment and finally said, "Oh, my God! Lancaster started the fentanyl crisis. He must have recruited Jeremy Monroe because he knew he was the Mayor's nephew. Then, at the right time, he threw him under the bus and killed him."

"Monroe was just a patsy," Peter said. "This Lancaster guy is ruthless. We need to be careful when we talk to him."

"Okay," Hannah said. "Let's have lunch, and then we'll talk to Tim and Ben."

They had lunch at a local diner and returned to the FBI office. They decided Tim and Ben would accompany them to the U.S. Bank building as backup.

They drove in separate vehicles and parked in the parking garage. They went inside and found a directory near the elevators. Lancaster Smith Development was near the top floor. Tim said he and Ben would monitor them from the floor below, so they got on the elevator and headed up. When they reached the floor below Lancaster's office, Hannah called Tim and placed her phone in her pocket so Tim and Ben could hear their conversation.

Hannah and Peter took the elevator up one more level. A directory pointed them to the left. The office of Lancaster Smith Development had two large glass doors that slid open into a beautiful, modern-looking reception area. An attractive young woman behind the reception desk greeted them with a smile. "Welcome to Lancaster Smith. How can I help you today?"

Hannah showed the woman her ID and said, "We need to speak with Edward Lancaster."

"Oh, okay. Just a minute," the woman said before walking toward the back offices.

After a minute, she returned and said, "Follow me."

They followed her down a hallway, and she opened the last door on the right before stepping aside to let them in. The office was enormous, with large windows on two walls that overlooked the city. Lancaster rose from his desk. He smiled, reached out his hand, and said. "Welcome. I'm Edward Lancaster."

Hannah and Peter shook his hand and introduced themselves. "Thank you for seeing us, Mr. Lancaster," Hannah said.

"Of course. Have a seat, please," Lancaster said, pointing to the two chairs in front of his desk. "How can I help you?"

"You have a beautiful view here," Peter said.

"It feels like heaven up here," Lancaster said.

"We need to ask you a few questions about Jeremy Monroe," Hannah said.

"Oh, yes. I was glad to learn his drug-trafficking days are over, but I don't know the man."

Hannah looked at Peter, who said, "Mr. Lancaster, how did you know the DEA would be raiding Monroe's pharmacy?"

Lancaster leaned back in his chair, smiled, and said, "I know because I provided the evidence to the DEA."

"That was you who sent the evidence anonymously?"

"That's right."

"Where did you get the evidence?"

"The drug problem was giving this city a terrible reputation, which is bad for business. It seemed the mayor was not giving the problem his full attention, so I hired a private detective to investigate it."

"Are you saying you're a good Samaritan?"

"No, I did it purely for business reasons."

"We have evidence that Jeremy Monroe visited you here. Did you facilitate his drug-making operation and then have him killed?"

Lancaster looked shocked at the question. "Are you accusing me of being responsible for the mess this city is in? That's ridiculous. I resent that accusation. I have never met Jeremy Monroe and have no idea why he was here. Perhaps he visited another office in this building."

Peter and Hannah looked at each other, surprised. Peter looked back at Lancaster and asked, "Are you saying you are entirely innocent regarding the drug crisis in this city?"

"That is exactly what I'm saying," Lancaster said. "I have only tried to help this city."

Hannah spoke up and said, "Thank you so much for your time, Mr. Lancaster."

She stood and practically pulled Peter out of Lancaster's office. As they waited for the elevator, Peter ran his hand through his hair and said, "What the hell just happened?"

Hannah shook her head. "I don't know."

They rode the elevator down one floor and met up with Tim and Ben. Tim asked, "What happened in there? Do you think Lancaster is really innocent?"

"It doesn't make any sense," Peter said. "I thought for sure he was behind all of this."

"I think he was lying," Hannah said. "I don't know how, but I can't believe all of that bullshit he said in there was true. Perhaps he is immune to Peter like I am."

"Why would he be immune?" Peter asked. "I'm pretty sure he's not a child of mine."

"I don't know," Hannah said. "There is definitely something off about the guy, though. He seemed way too smug."

After Hannah and Peter left his office, Lancaster pushed a button on his desk. Ten seconds later, Landa entered his office. "What's going on, Boss?"

"That FBI woman and her gifted partner are getting too close. We need to do something about them."

"It will be my pleasure."

Chapter 15

It was getting late when they left the U.S. Bank Center, and everyone decided to meet again in the morning. Hannah picked up her car at the FBI office and drove Peter home. On the way, she received a text. It showed on her car's monitor that it was from her mom. She clicked on it, and a female voice read it. "Hi, Honey. I need you to come here as soon as you can. It's urgent."

"I wonder what that's about," Hannah said.

"I don't know. Call her and ask," Peter said.

Hannah dialed her mom's number. It rang four times and then went to voicemail. Hannah looked at Peter. "Do you mind if I take you home later?"

"Not at all. Let's go see what's up with your mom."

When they arrived at Michelle's house, there was a car in the driveway that they didn't recognize. "Oh, she has company," Hannah said. "I wonder who would be visiting her."

Hannah parked on the street behind the driveway. They got out and walked past the car toward the front door. As they passed the car, Peter said, "Didn't Tim say the guy who threw that mannequin at us had a dark blue Malibu?"

Hannah's eyes widened. "That's right." She pulled her gun out and said, "Stay behind me."

Hannah turned the knob on the front door. It was unlocked. She quietly opened the door and went inside. She motioned for Peter to wait. As she approached the living room, she noticed Peter was following closely behind her. She waved at him to go back, but he shook his head, so she gave up and continued forward. When she reached the living room, she looked right and saw Michelle bound to a chair and gagged. Her eyes were wide with fear.

"Mom!" She gasped and rushed toward her.

A man stepped into view, gun raised, the barrel trained on Michelle's head. "Stop where you are," he said. The man was Victor Landa.

Hannah pointed her gun at him. "Drop it!" she said.

"It is you who needs to drop the gun," Landa said. "I'm sure you don't want to have to clean your mother's brains off the wall."

Hannah hesitated and then said, "Fine. I'm putting it down. Don't shoot."

She bent down slowly, put the gun on the floor, then stood up again. She kept her elbows down but raised her hands. "Thank you," Landa said as he raised his gun at Hannah and fired.

Michelle screamed through her gag as Peter instinctively leaped in front of Hannah. The bullet entered his side. He fell to the floor, hitting his head on the coffee table. The rest seemed to happen in slow motion. He watched Hannah bend down and pick up her gun. As she stood, she quickly pointed her gun at Landa. Without taking the time to aim, she fired at the same time Landa did. Her bullet clipped his left arm, while Landa's bullet hit Hanna just above her stomach. She fell to the ground next to Peter. Landa then pointed his gun at Michelle.

"Stop!" Peter yelled.

To his amazement, Landa froze.

He remembered what Michelle had told him about his other ability. "Get out of here!" he ordered.

Landa started to leave, but Peter had a better idea. "Wait!" he said. "Put the gun down, find a police officer, and confess everything you have done."

Landa set his gun on the floor and walked out of the house. Peter turned to Hannah. She was breathing hard. He remembered his watch. It had a special panic button. He pushed it. He then put a hand on Hannah's face and said, "Help is on the way."

Hannah shook her head weakly. "It's too late," she whispered, each word a struggle. "You should know I'm happy I finally met my dad." A faint smile appeared on her face. "You really are an angel. Of that, I have no doubt." Her breathing grew shallower, each breath more labored than the last. Then, silence. Her eyes, once full of life, now seemed empty.

Peter's hands trembled as he gently closed her eyes. Then, as if the weight of the world had come crashing down on him, he threw his head back and screamed, "Noooooooooooo!"

After taking a deep breath, he looked up again, his voice hoarse as he shouted toward the heavens, "Aziel! I know you are listening! I need you! Don't ignore me!"

Suddenly, the room became a blur, and then a bright light caused Peter's eyelids to snap shut. Even with his eyes closed, the brightness was almost overwhelming. When the light dimmed, Peter opened his eyes. Aziel stood before him. He no longer wore the clothes of a priest but was clad in a long, flowing robe made of white linen, which seemed to glow with a radiant light.

Without a word, Aziel held out his hand for Peter, who took it and stood up. Peter looked down at his side where Landa had shot him. His shirt was bloodied and had a hole in it, but his skin was clean and untouched. He pressed on the area but felt no pain. He looked at Aziel, "How is this possible?"

Aziel put his hand on Peter's head and said, "Remember."

Suddenly, a flood of memories surged through him. He saw his celestial past. He remembered his life as an angel. He recalled the purpose that brought him to Earth. He remembered falling in love with Michelle. He remembered the punishment that tore it all away. He also remembered his close friendship with Aziel, the one constant in both of his lives.

Aziel's voice was steady and unwavering. "God has decided to end your punishment, Micah. It is time for you to return to your duties."

Peter looked down at Hannah. "What about her? You can help her."

"It is her time," Aziel said.

"No, it is not. I remember why God sent me here. It was because of Lancaster. He's responsible for this. This wasn't a natural death. You can save her."

Aziel shook his head. "I don't think so. This is what got you in trouble the last time."

"Please, Aziel. I beg you."

Aziel looked up for several seconds, then looked back at Peter. "Okay," he said, "but there is a price. You will have to give up being an angel. This time, it will be forever."

"I've done it before. I can do it again."

"You will also again lose all memory of your angel life."

"Yes! Yes! Anything! I don't care. Just help her."

"This will be the last time we speak, Micah. I can no longer help you. I wish you luck in your new life."

Suddenly, the room became very bright again, and then there was darkness.

"Peter. Peter."

Peter opened his eyes. He saw Hannah kneeling over him on his right and Michelle on his left. He sat up and looked at Hannah. He smiled the biggest smile of his life. "You're okay! Oh, thank God!"

The sound of sirens erupted outside as Peter hugged Hannah. "I thought you were dead. How are you okay?"

"You don't remember?" Michelle asked.

"Remember what?"

"You called your angel friend, Aziel, and asked for his help."

"Really? Did you see him?" Peter asked.

"No, but you did. I heard you talking to him, but I only heard your side of the conversation. You made a bargain with him. I don't know what that was, but it sounded like you gave up everything for Hannah."

Peter looked at Hannah and said, "I don't know what I gave up, but I'm sure I got the better end of the deal."

They hugged again, and Hannah said, "I love you, Dad."

Peter smiled as several police officers came through the door, guns drawn. Two of them stopped and pointed their weapons at Hannah, Michelle, and Peter, while two more continued to check the rest of the house. One of the police officers asked, "Is one of you the homeowner?"

"That would be me? My name is Michelle Meyers," Michelle said.

"Can I see your identification?" the officer asked.

"It's in the bedroom," Michelle said.

"Wait a minute," Hannah said. "I'm her daughter. I'm Special Agent Hannah Meyers with the FBI."

She started to stand up, but the officer put his hand up and said, "Slowly."

She stood slowly and took out her identification from her pocket. That's when the officer noticed the blood on her shirt. He lowered his gun and said, "Oh, shit. Have you been shot?"

Hannah looked down at her shirt and said, "It's a long story, but I'm okay."

Peter stood up, also covered in blood. The officer looked at him and said, "What the hell happened here?"

"Everything is okay now," Peter said. "Someone we were investigating broke in and took Michelle hostage, but he's gone now. He went to turn himself in."

The other officer looked at his partner. "Now I've seen it all."

The other two officers returned. One of them said, "The house is clear. We'll let the paramedics know it's safe to come in."

"Tell them they're not needed," Hannah said.

Seeing the blood, the officer said, "Are you sure?"

"Yes. We're fine," Hannah said.

Tim and Ben entered the house. They showed their IDs to the officers and came into the living room. Upon seeing Hannah and Peter, Ben said, "Are you guys okay? What happened?"

"Landa was here," Hannah said. "He took my mom hostage to draw us here."

"For what purpose?" Tim asked.

"We were getting too close. I'm sure his job was to eliminate us."

"But Lancaster told you he was innocent. Do you think he was able to lie to you?" Ben asked.

"I was pretty sure he was able to lie before," Hannah said. "Now I'm positive."

"That's a lot of blood," Tim said. "How are you two okay?"

Hannah looked at Peter and then back at Tim, "You'll never believe it."

"An angel saved them," Michelle said.

"What?" Tim asked. "Did you say an angel saved them?"

"That's right," Michelle said.

Tim looked at Hannah, who said, "I told you that you wouldn't believe it."

"I don't know," Tim said. "A year ago, I would not have believed that a list of special people even existed, much less one who people couldn't lie to. Believing in angels seems like a small step now, relatively speaking."

"I don't know what really happened," Hannah said. "All I know is Peter took a bullet for me. Unfortunately, Landa still shot me. I felt my life slipping away. Then I woke up perfectly fine. I untied Mom, and we woke Peter up. He was fine, too. If it wasn't divine intervention, then I have no idea how to explain it."

"We're just happy you guys are okay," Ben said. "What happened to Landa?"

Peter looked at Hanna and then back at Ben. "Well, it seems I have one other ability I wasn't aware of. By now, hopefully, Landa is spilling his guts to the police."

Ben shook his head. "This is unbelievable. What do we do about Lancaster now?"

Upon hearing the name, Michelle's interest seemed to peak. "You've mentioned that name a couple of times. I heard Micah say it when he talked to Aziel."

Peter looked at Michelle. "Really? What did I say about him?"

"You said he was the reason you were sent here. Who is he?"

"He is someone who we think might be behind the fentanyl crisis we've been investigating," Peter said.

Michelle slowly nodded. "I see. It all makes sense now."

"What makes sense?" Peter asked. "Do you know something about Lancaster?"

"Well, I don't know anything about Lancaster, but I know why you were here on Earth."

Tim and Ben looked at each other, a confused expression on their faces.

"Why was I here on Earth?" Peter asked.

"You were a demon hunter. Demons sometimes pretend to be human. They have always been jealous of God's love for humans, so they take pleasure in causing chaos whenever and wherever they can. Your job was to expose them. Once you did, they would have no choice but to return to Hell or set up shop elsewhere. The problem with starting over for them is that it takes time to build up power and influence."

"Was I hunting this Lancaster when I met you?"

"I don't know. You called him 'Luthanis' at the time. Maybe he adopted a human name."

"Wait a minute," Tim said. "This is starting to get really weird. Are you saying Lancaster is a demon and Peter here is some kind of..."

"Angel," Michelle said.

"Angel?" Tim repeated.

"Former angel," Peter said. "That's the prevailing theory."

Tim ran a hand through his hair. "I don't know if I believe in angels and demons, but let's suppose it's true. What do we do about Lancaster?"

"You simply need to expose him, and he will disappear," Michelle said.

Hanna's phone rang. She looked at the screen. It was a local number that she didn't recognize. She tapped the answer button and said, "This is Special Agent Meyers."

"Agent Meyers. This is Captain Garcia."

Hannah put the call on speaker and said, "Oh, yes, Captain. I'm here with my partners. What can I do for you?"

"A couple of my officers have a man named Victor Landa in custody. He has confessed to numerous crimes, including kidnapping your mother and killing you. I wanted to confirm his story, but it seems you are alive and well, which I am very pleased about."

"Thank you, Captain. I'm happy about that, too. Landa did kidnap my Mom, and he tried to kill Peter and me. Thankfully, he failed. Did he say anything about Edward Lancaster?"

"Oh, yes. He said Lancaster ordered your executions. He also said Lancaster helped Monroe get started making fentanyl and provided him with some of the ingredients he needed. In addition, according to Landa, he ordered him to kill Monroe."

Tim spoke up, "Hello, Captain. I'm Special Agent Timothy Carter. It seems the Mexican drug cartels were not involved in this case after all. Lancaster set everything up to remove Monroe from office so he could proceed with his real estate project. That means we can no longer justify our involvement in this case. Lancaster is all yours. We would like to see this through, though. Do you think you can give us a heads-up so we can be there when you make an arrest?"

"I think that's a reasonable request. We're putting together a case now."

"We'll be happy to share what we know," Tim said.

"Every little bit helps," Garcia said. "We should have a warrant sometime tomorrow morning."

When Hannah hung up, she looked at Michelle and said, "Mom, you seem to know more about what is happening than we do. I don't understand why Lancaster needed people to do his dirty work. If he has the power to influence people's behavior, why couldn't he influence the mayor's behavior and make him approve his project?"

"Just like with Micah, his influence only works on the wicked. The more evil one has in his heart, the easier it is for an angel, or demon, to influence his behavior."

"Okay, then why didn't Lancaster kill Monroe himself, or Peter and me, for that matter, instead of sending Landa? I would think a demon could kill without remorse."

"Angels are forbidden to kill humans," Michelle said. "Since demons are fallen angels, that rule also applies to them."

"I'm sorry. That doesn't make sense," Ben said. "If demons are angels who rebelled against God, they are basically criminals. Since when do criminals care about rules?"

"I can't answer that," Michelle said. "Everything I know about angels and demons I learned from Micah, and I'm sure he told me only a fraction of what he knows, or knew. I do know that some bad people think of themselves as righteous. Perhaps even demons have a code of honor. I don't know."

Chapter 16

Hannah picked up Peter the following morning. When he got in her car, she said, "Well, Dad, this is it. Tomorrow, you can get back to your normal life."

"It feels good to hear the name, 'Dad.'"

Hannah leaned over and kissed Peter on the cheek. "I think you earned it, Dad."

"So, what's the plan for today?"

"We plan to meet the police outside the U.S. Bank Center at ten. They will arrest Lancaster, and we can put this case behind us."

"I don't know if I believe Lancaster is a demon, but if he is, do you think a jail will hold him?" Peter asked.

"You would know that better than I. It's too bad you can't remember. I guess we will see."

They met Tim and Ben and drove to the U.S. Bank Center. There, they met Captain Garcia and four police officers. They all rode the elevator to the top floor together. It was a tight squeeze, but they managed it.

The officers entered Lancaster's office first, followed by the FBI agents. "We're here to see Edward Lancaster," Garcia told the receptionist.

"I'm afraid he didn't come in this morning," she said.

Garcia told the officers to search the place, and they divided into pairs. They thoroughly searched each room. After several minutes, they returned and told the captain they had found no sign of Lancaster.

Garcia took out his phone and dialed a number. "Did you find him?" he asked when the phone was answered. He listened for several seconds and said, "Okay, thanks."

He hung up the phone and said, "We had another team searching his home. It seems Lancaster has disappeared."

"That's what Mom said would happen," Hannah said to Peter.

The receptionist called out, "Excuse me. Is one of you gentlemen named Peter Beckett?"

"That's me," Peter said.

She held up a box and said, "This is for you." It was about the size and shape of a shoe box and wrapped in paper printed with the word "Congratulations," which repeated every few inches.

Peter took the box from the woman, and Tim said, "Be careful! It could be rigged."

"I don't think so," Peter said, "but you are welcome to back away if you want." Nobody moved, and Peter ripped the paper off the box. In his hand was a wooden keepsake box. He shook his head, saying, "I don't believe it."

"What is it?" Hannah asked.

"I made this box. I sold several of these online years ago."

"How did Lancaster get it?" Tim asked.

"I don't know. He probably ordered it from me."

Peter opened the box and took out a small, hand-carved palm tree. He held it up. "I made this, too. Lancaster must have been keeping tabs on me."

"So he's known all these years who you are," Hannah said.

"It would seem so."

"Why do you think he gave that to you now?" Tim asked.

"I suppose it's his way of saying goodbye. Perhaps he is moving to someplace tropical, with palm trees, and this is an invitation to come and look for him."

"Why would he do that?" Ben asked. "Wouldn't he want to start over without any interference?"

"Maybe he enjoys the challenge. No true champion wants to compete against amateurs."

"But he's starting from zero," Ben said. "He needs to work his way up to champion status again."

Captain Garcia, who had been listening, spoke up. "He's not starting from zero. We checked his records, and he had very little money in the bank. Other than his house and his shares in the company, we assume most of his wealth is in offshore bank accounts."

"I don't care," Peter said. "He's someone else's problem now." He put his arm around Hannah. "I have a family that I have neglected for far too long."

Epilogue

Three months later, the man formerly known as Edward Lancaster stood in front of his new South Beach nightclub in Miami. The woman tasked with managing the place stood beside him as they watched two workers install a new sign on the building. She was the ideal woman to manage the nightclub. She was young, pretty, intelligent, and easily influenced. Best of all, she coincidentally had a name he found perfect for the job.

"What do you think, Hannah?" he asked.

"I like it, Mr. Lucian, but I'm curious. Why did you name this place Micah's?"

"I named it after an old adversary who was forced into early retirement."

She smiled. "I see. You are rubbing it in his face."

"Oh, no. This is more of an invitation for him to get back into the game."

"Why would you want that?"

"I crave the challenge."

"I'm sure plenty of people on South Beach can challenge you."

"No, they can't. Not like Micah."

I truly appreciate you taking the time to read Truth Be Told. I hope you enjoyed the story.

I would be incredibly grateful if you left a review on Amazon, Goodreads, or wherever you purchased this book. Your thoughts help other readers discover the series and mean a lot to me as an author. Whether it's a few words or a detailed review, your feedback makes a difference.

Thank you again for your support. I couldn't do this without readers like you.

Charles Huss

Don't miss out!

Visit the website below and you can sign up to receive emails whenever Charles Huss publishes a new book. There's no charge and no obligation.

https://books2read.com/r/B-A-LHRY-JULMG

BOOKS 2 READ

Connecting independent readers to independent writers.

Did you love *Truth Be Told*? Then you should read *The Last Healer*[1] by Charles Huss!

[2]

On the eve of her thirtieth birthday, Katie, a television news reporter, unhappy with her career and her love life, decides to spend the weekend alone at a Wisconsin ski resort.

Joe is a man content to live a private life in his cabin in the woods. Since the death of his wife, he has avoided intimate relationships and prefers to keep a low profile to prevent people from learning of his unusual abilities.

On the way to the ski resort, Katie makes a wrong turn during a snowstorm and hits Joe with her car. Lost and with no

---

1. https://books2read.com/u/3yQJ0B

2. https://books2read.com/u/3yQJ0B

cell signal, Katie tries to keep Joe alive until she can get help. During Joe's recovery, Katie learns his secret and soon helps to investigate his family's mysterious past while Joe helps Katie investigate a double murder. Love blossoms while they slowly unravel both mysteries, but danger lies ahead. Can Joe discover the full extent of his abilities before it is too late?

The Last Healer is part mystery, part romance, and part science fiction. It is a book that can be enjoyed in just a few hours but remembered for a lifetime.

Read more at charleshuss.com.

Also by Charles Huss

Last Healer Mysteries
Last Chance
Last Flight
The Last Healer
Last Rites

Standalone
Identity Crisis
Falling Star
Saving Apollo
Truth Be Told

Watch for more at charleshuss.com.

About the Author

Charles Huss was born and raised in the suburbs of Chicago but has lived most of his adult life in the Tampa Bay, Florida area. He is a graduate of St. Petersburg College and is the writer of several blogs. He currently lives with his wife, Rose, and their three cats.

Read more at charleshuss.com.